BUT NOT FORLORN

A Clint Wolf Novel
(Book 7)

BY

BJ BOURG

WWW.BJBOURG.COM

TITLES BY BJ BOURG

LONDON CARTER MYSTERY SERIES

James 516

Proving Grounds

Silent Trigger

Bullet Drop

Elevation

Blood Rise

CLINT WOLF MYSTERY SERIES

But Not Forgotten

But Not Forgiven

But Not Forsaken

But Not Forever

But Not For Naught

But Not Forbidden

But Not Forlorn

But Not Formidable

BUT NOT FORLORN
A Clint Wolf Novel by BJ Bourg

This book is a work of fiction.
All names, characters, locations, and incidents are products of the
author's imagination, or have been used fictitiously.
Any resemblance to actual persons living or dead, locales, or events
is entirely coincidental.

Cover design by Christine Savoie of Bayou Cover Designs

PUBLISHED IN THE UNITED STATES OF AMERICA

CHAPTER 1

Sunday, April 23
Mechant Loup-North

As he gave his campaign speech, Lance Beaman scanned the faces of the Mechant Loup-North residents who had gathered at the home of Chet Robichaux, his old friend and client. He was better at one-on-one interaction, and he tried to focus on the people with whom he'd connected during the meet-and-greet.

There were a few nods as he began his speech—mostly when he spoke about his many years in real estate and how he had spent a lifetime in the area helping locals realize their dreams of becoming homeowners—but no one seemed especially enthusiastic.

"I plan on bringing real change to Mechant Loup, just like I did with the development of Mechant Loup-North." A few nods here and there. He had been instrumental in developing the subdivision north of the Mechant Loup Bridge, and it had helped bring in a new flavor of people from all across the country, most of them retirees searching for a final resting spot that was quiet and safe. The majority of the people in the room were among those who had relocated here within the past year. According to Chet, they had already established residency and registered to vote, and were all self-described *hardcore voters* who voted in every election. "I'm going to revamp the police department and make sure our children and schools are safe!"

Could the polls be wrong? Lance wondered, the tightness returning to his chest as he surveyed the unenthusiastic crowd. According to his consultant, he was eleven points ahead of Pauline

Cain in the race for mayor, but it appeared he wasn't carrying two percent of this room. He adjusted his collar. He could feel the sweat dripping down his back and he cursed his choice of wardrobe—slacks, long-sleeve button-down shirt, and sports jacket. *Why aren't they applauding my speech? Doesn't everyone want school security and child safety?*

It suddenly dawned on him—hardly any of these people had school-aged children, so they didn't care as much about school safety as a younger crowd might. "You know, people, I hope to retire someday." He pulled the microphone away from his face and made a show of studying each and every person's face, nodding vigorously as he did so. When he spoke again, he raised his voice a little. "Apparently, retirement makes you look twenty years younger. I mean, judging by the looks of you handsome devils with your beautiful better halves, it certainly does."

That brought an initial chuckle from an old man who sat at a table to his left, and that caused a few others to laugh.

"Well, I hope to look as good as y'all do someday." He nodded and pursed his lips. "But it'll be a while yet for me, because I've still got some work to do. As you all know, people want to retire to a place where their dollar stretches a lot farther and where they can leave their doors unlocked if they want." He paused and studied the expressions on their faces. His message seemed to be resonating better. "You each want a mayor who will do everything he can to keep your property safe, and someone you can talk to if you have a problem—any problem."

Applause sounded from the back of the room and it spread like a wave. Lance smiled to himself. *I'm finally getting somewhere with this group.*

"I'm the only mayor with the integrity to hold the police department's feet to the fire. I'll make sure they crack down on criminals and drug dealers, while leaving the good citizens alone. The drunks you often see roaming around town as you walk the strip, and the drug dealers who are operating in the shadows of our beautiful landscape"—he raised his left fist and turned his outstretched thumb downward—"they're all about to have a rude awakening, because when I become mayor, I'm bringing my whip and I'm cracking down on them all!"

More applause.

Lance took a breath and wiped sweat from his bare dome. "You know, I hate to say it, but we can't expect our current mayor to be tough on crime. I'm sure you've all seen my commercials…"

Nearly every head nodded and a low murmur of approval spread across the room. One man, a well-groomed fellow wearing a fancy suit with a red tie, stood at the back of the room. Lance had noticed him earlier and the man seemed indifferent during most of his speech. Now, though, at the mention of the town's current mayor, the man's face had hardened and he glowered at Lance. Trying not to show his uneasiness, Lance looked away and found a friendlier face at the front of the room, continued.

"How can we trust a mayor to be tough on crime when her husband, Hays Cain, was involved in all kinds of shady business?" When he mentioned Pauline Cain's late husband, several men in the room booed. His voice began to grow with excitement as more and more people began to verbalize their disdain for Hays Cain. "Some might say he was a victim, but we all know he was involved in illegal activity of the highest order, and there's no way his wife was not aware of his wrongdoings.

"Me, I'm going to rid this town of all criminal elements and I'm going to begin with Pauline Cain. Once she's out of the way, I'm going to run every other criminal out of our town. They will know there's no place for them here. They won't work here, they won't visit here, and they won't live here. They will not be welcome here and I will make damn sure they know it!" The room erupted in applause and cheers. He stole a glance in the direction of the man at the back of the room. His eyes were mere slits and his jaw was set. Lance quickly looked away and continued. "In closing, I ask you to please join my team and help me spread my message about safety and security, so we can make this town the best place on earth to retire."

The room erupted again, but once the noise had subsided, a woman waved from the corner of the room. "What did you mean about my dollars stretching a lot farther?"

"I'm glad you brought that up." Lance wiped his hands on his slacks. "Yep, I'm going to make sure the town council never raises your taxes above the current rate."

"What about property taxes?" the woman pressed.

"I will do everything in my power as mayor to make sure your property taxes never go up," Lance lied. "And that's a promise you can take to the bank!"

Before anyone else could ask another question in front of the group, he waved and placed the microphone on a nearby chair. Chet rushed forward to rescue him, snatched up the mic. "Thank y'all for coming to our meet-and-greet," Chet said loudly. "Please dig deep into your wallets and purses and consider making the maximum donation allowed by law. We need your help to put this town back on the right path, and it begins right here and right now."

Lance stood and smiled as he watched men pull out their wallets and women dig into their purses. He recognized many of them, because he had closed the deal on most of their homes in Mechant Loup-North, and they had all been pleased with their purchases. Most of the attendees filed into a rough line and stopped to hand him their contributions and to say goodbye on their way out the door. He felt like a priest bidding his congregation farewell at the end of mass. It made him feel powerful. A few people slipped out the back, and he figured they were too embarrassed to admit they didn't have enough money to help out. He didn't mind, though, as their vote was more important than anything else.

Once the majority of the crowd had gone, Lance visited with Chet for a few minutes before calling it an evening himself. "I want to thank you for putting on this event," Lance said, stopping in the doorway to shake hands with his friend. A thought suddenly occurred to him and he looked around, wondering what had become of the stranger at the back of the room. "Say, Chet, did you notice the well-dressed man at the back of the room?"

"They were all well-dressed. Can you narrow it down a bit more?"

"He wore the red tie."

"Hmm, I can't say that I noticed anyone in a red tie." Chet scowled. "Why? Is there something wrong?"

Lance shrugged. "It's nothing, I guess. He just didn't seem like a supporter is all."

"Yeah, well, you won't get a hundred percent of the vote, that's for sure. Pauline Cain is popular in some circles, but then you knew this would be an uphill battle."

Lance thanked his friend again and walked down the cobblestone steps and strode across the smooth driveway. His car was parked a few dozen feet from the door, and he groaned as the Louisiana heat enveloped him. It wasn't summer yet but it was already hot. His short legs pumped like pistons as he hurried to his car. He stripped his jacket off before he reached the car and tossed it in the back seat as soon as he opened the driver door. He cursed the stifling heat that enveloped him when he took his seat.

"Hurry up, damn it!" he said, twisting the key in the ignition and turning the blower on the air conditioner as high as it could go. The air that initially blew through the vent was smothering, but he knew it would only last for a minute or so. He left his door open while waiting for the air to cool, glanced back toward Chet's place. The sun was setting behind the house and the shadows in the front yard were starting to grow long. He had one more stop to make before heading home.

Finally, the air from the vents cooled and he slammed his door. He glanced up and paused with his hand on the gearshift. *What the hell?* He leaned forward and squinted, unable to comprehend fully what he was seeing. Just to the left and front of where he was parked, a clump of thick trees grew at the center of the boulevard. From the shadows of those trees, a man wearing a hooded mask emerged and stood directly in front of his car, blocking his way. The man approached slowly, menacingly. There was a satchel over the man's left shoulder and he was holding some sort of bottle in his right hand.

In a state of panic, Lance began fumbling with the gearshift, trying to find *reverse*. Before he could get it in gear in time, the man touched off a lighter and lit a wick that extended from the bottle. In one deft motion, he then launched the bottle directly at the front windshield of Lance's car, aiming for the driver side. Flame immediately exploded across the windshield and onto the hood.

Letting out a terrified scream, Lance fumbled some more with the shift and it finally fell into place. He smashed the accelerator and his vehicle shot backward. When he'd backed up enough, he smashed the brakes, but the pedal felt spongy and his vehicle barely slowed. Suddenly, it slammed to a stop and his head jerked violently with the collision. A quick glance in his rearview mirror told him all he needed to know—he'd plowed into a large pickup truck that belonged to Chet's son.

Before he could do anything else, a second bottle exploded across the windshield and the flames grew higher. Smoke began to seep into the cab. Due to the flames and smoke, he could no longer see the man, but he knew he was still out there somewhere.

"What do you want?" he screamed as loud as he could, shoving the gearshift in *drive*. He shot a glance toward the house. There was no sign of life. Although it was futile to scream for help, he did so anyway. "Somebody help me!"

A third bottle exploded into the rear windshield and the glass shattered, allowing the accelerant and fire to gush into the back seat. He was in real danger now and needed to get away. Locking the gearshift in *drive*, he shot forward, driving blind, trying to remember where the center of the boulevard was located. If he misjudged the route, he would end up in the trees and feed the already growing flames that were threatening to completely envelope his car.

Swerving violently as he sped forward, Lance let out a terrifying cry when he caught a glimpse of the mystery man, who was poised to throw another bottle at his car—and this one was heading straight for the window on the front passenger door. Before the car could speed out of range, the bottle smashed through the side window and a fiery ball gushed into the opening and cloaked Lance in its hellish embrace.

Lance didn't know if his car was moving or not—and, at that moment, he didn't really care. The pain and heat that wrapped over him was so intense it shocked him to his soul. He couldn't even scream. When he opened his mouth in the blaze, the only noise that came out was a guttural moan, and the insides of his lips and tongue felt as though a cup of molten lava had been forced down his throat.

As Lance struggled to suck in small amounts of heated breath at a time, he was vaguely aware of the driver's side window being smashed open and another wave of fire gushing over him. Somehow, above the roar of the flames, he heard a strong voice calling out to him, "For you have sown the wind, you piece of shit, now reap the whirlwind!"

CHAPTER 2

Clint and Susan Wolf's house…

I rolled onto my back and stretched long and hard, letting out an animalistic growl as I did so.

"You woke the neighbors with all of that noise." Susan sat up next to me in bed, her right breast poking out of the side of her tank top.

"We don't have neighbors."

"Exactly my point." She adjusted her shirt and tucked her breast away, which brought a frown to my face. She noticed and cocked her head to the side, pushed a lock of brown hair behind an ear. "You'll be getting to spend a lot of time with her in the next hundred, or so, years—that is, unless you grow tired of me now that we're an old married couple."

"Old married couple?" I laughed. We had gotten married on a cruise ship last Sunday. After the wedding, we had sailed from New Orleans to Jamaica, then the Grand Caymans, and then Cozumel. We had returned just this afternoon, a little after one, and had taken a long nap, neither of us wanting our vacation together to end. "We've only been married—what?—five minutes?"

"I noticed how you avoided that whole question."

"I didn't avoid anything." I brushed my fingers lightly across her strong and tanned leg. "I'll never grow tired of you, Susan Wilson."

"It's Susan *Wolf* now, Mr. Man." Susan straddled me and leaned her arms against my chest, studying my brown eyes with her own. "And I'll never grow tired of you, Clint Wolf."

I'd known I was in love with Susan for quite some time and I had always felt very close to her, but I was surprised how much closer I felt after spending the last seven days with her—and how much I'd learned about her. It was the first real time we'd spent together talking about things other than criminal cases or fighting or our family or the shelter Susan was running for battered women.

One of the things that surprised me about her was that she was afraid of frogs. She had told me over dinner one night in the cruise ship's dining room that the fear stemmed from an incident that happened when she was a little girl.

"There were these cute red boots I used to wear every time it rained. I'd go prancing around in the ankle-deep water, thinking I ruled the world. Well, this one day, the ditches had flooded and I was in a hurry to get outside. I rushed to the carport, kicked off my sandals, and shoved my right foot directly into the boot." She had paused to shudder and cover her face. "There was a frog at the bottom of my boot. I have no idea how it got in there, but I just remember it feeling all slimy and cold between my toes—"

"Wait—between your toes?" I'd asked, incredulous.

She'd shuddered again and her face had twisted into a grimace as she nodded. "I smashed the life right out of that little frog. All of its guts squirted up between my toes. It was the grossest thing I've ever experienced. I was gagging and hopping around trying so hard to get the boot off that I fell and skinned both my knees." She had paused to take a sip of water and I'd wondered if she was having trouble keeping her appetizer down. "The only way I'll wear rubber boots now is if I throw them around first, so anything inside can come out."

As I thought back to the conversation now, and the way I'd pictured a child-size version of my wife hopping around on one leg and gagging, I broke out laughing. Susan, who was still straddling me, began pouting. "What's so funny? I want to know so I can laugh, too."

I tried to stop laughing long enough to tell her, but it was no use. Each time I thought I had it under control, I'd imagine her little face all freaked out and would picture her hopping desperately around, and I'd break out again. It took a long three or four minutes for me to finally calm down enough to say, "Boots—the frog in your boots."

Her mouth dropped open. "Hey, that's not funny! I was traumatized."

Although she tried to pretend to be upset, she also started laughing, and soon fell to the bed beside me. We were laughing so hard at first that we didn't hear the phones ringing. When we finally stopped and lay there exhausted and happy, Susan shot up on an elbow and glanced around the room. "Did you hear that?"

I sobered up. "Hear what?"

"One of us has a voicemail. It's got to be work."

Susan was the chief of police for the town of Mechant Loup and I was the town's chief of detectives. We both served at the pleasure of the town's mayor, who was a widow named Pauline Cain, and we operated as equal and separate branches of the police department. The only difference between her chief title and my chief title was that she supervised three patrol officers and I supervised no one but myself.

While we had been on our cruise for the past seven days, the day-to-day police duties in town had fallen into the very capable hands of Susan's most senior officer, Melvin Saltzman, who normally worked one of the night shifts.

As for my relief, Sheriff Buck Turner had that covered. Turner was the sheriff of Chateau Parish and he had offered to have a detective on standby in case something happened while I was out of town. I had gratefully accepted the offer, and it helped to make my trip more relaxing. But now, we were back on duty, and it appeared duty might be calling.

Susan rolled off her side of the bed and began searching for her phone. I dropped my feet to the floor and stared at the luggage strewn about the room. After spending an hour outside with Achilles when we got back home, we had dragged our suitcases and bags of souvenirs upstairs and just dropped them wherever we were standing and then ripped each other's clothes off and got back to spending quality time together.

I'd never seen our room in such disarray and didn't even know where to start searching for my phone. "Do you see my phone?" I asked, snatching the nearest bag and opening it. "I thought I put it in that triangle bag."

Susan was on her hands and knees on the opposite side of the bed and I couldn't even see her. Finally, I heard her triumphant cry. "Got it!" Her head popped up at the foot of the bed and she fumbled with the phone, pulled it to her ear to hear the voicemail. Her mouth was partially open as she listened to the message. I just sat there and stared. She looked beautiful in her tank top and nothing else, with the phone pressed to her head, concentrating on what was being said. Of course, she could make an oyster sack look good—

"What is it?" I asked when I saw her eyes widen and her mouth clamp shut. She didn't immediately answer. After a few seconds, she slowly pulled the phone from her ear and ended the voicemail. She stared down at her hands for a long moment and then looked up at me, her face a shade or two lighter.

"The honeymoon's over."

"Why?" My mind raced. "Who was it? What's going on?"

"Someone set fire to mayoral candidate Lance Beaman." She swallowed hard. "They burned him to death in his car."

It took a moment for the information to process. When it did, my own eyes widened. "Oh, that's convenient."

Susan nodded slowly, a blank expression on her face, and I knew she was thinking the same thing I was thinking.

CHAPTER 3

After Susan and I had hurried into our clothes and jumped into her marked cruiser, I called the office to find out more information. Beth Gandy, who was our weekend dispatcher, answered on the first ring.

"Clint, thank God y'all are back in town! What on earth is happening to this place?"

"What more can you tell me?" I asked.

"Well, I received a call at seven thirty-seven from a man screaming for help. He said that Lance Beaman had crashed into the curb near some trees and was burning up inside his car and they couldn't get to him. I dispatched Melvin and contacted the fire department. They were all there within minutes…"

She stopped talking to answer Melvin on the police radio. After letting him know Susan and I were en route, she got back on the phone with me. "Once they got there, Melvin said he could smell an accelerant. He believes it's arson…he believes someone intentionally burned Mr. Beaman to death."

"Can you call the state fire marshal's office?"

"Already done. They've got a marshal en route as we speak."

"Thanks, Beth." I ended the call and jerked my seatbelt on as Susan smashed the gas pedal and we shot across town, heading north. The sun was rapidly descending in the westward sky and darkness would be here soon. I glanced sideways at Susan. Her jaw was set and the orange glow from the sun sparkled in her dark eyes. "You do know who his supporters will accuse of doing this, right?"

Susan continued staring straight ahead. "What if she *is* responsible?"

I sighed and rubbed my forehead. The race for mayor had grown contentious and Beaman had said some awful things about Pauline Cain, but I didn't think she was capable of murdering someone simply to keep her job. "I just hope we solve it right away. If this thing drags out until election day, there's no telling what'll happen."

"And what if solving it means she did it?"

"I don't even want to think she's capable of burning a man to death." Not only was Pauline Cain a good boss and a great town leader, but she had also helped me out on a personal matter when Susan was in trouble. I owed her big. I didn't want to repay her by doubting her and accusing her of murder.

"Not only do you have to *think* she's capable of doing it, but you also have to ready yourself for the possibility of having to arrest her for doing it."

I knew Susan was right, but I wasn't ready to go there in my mind. "Let's just get to the scene and see what we've got. Maybe there's a perfectly good explanation for what happened."

Susan cocked her head to the side. "And what could possibly be a good explanation for burning a man alive?"

I only stared out the passenger's side window and waited as she drove. It barely took a minute for us to reach the Mechant Loup Bridge, and, before long, we were zipping through the Mechant Loup-North neighborhood. I saw red and blues flashing brightly in the waning light of the day and pointed up ahead. "It's way at the back."

Susan cut the steering wheel to the left and cruised down the street until we saw a large house set far back from the main boulevard, which was called North Boulevard. It was the biggest house in the area and it rose up from the ground like a mountain on the horizon. I hesitated to call it a house. A more accurate descriptor would be *mansion*. It was two stories tall, but each story must've had twelve-foot ceilings. The windows that lined the front of the house were at least eight feet tall, and the bright light that glowed from inside lit up the front yard like the daytime.

However, as bright as the lights were, their glow did not quite reach the portion of the driveway farthest from the house, and it was in these shadows that we spotted the smoldering remains of what was supposed to be Lance Beaman's car. Dark smoke lifted from the wreckage and drifted away on the soft breeze, and I wondered if one of the tufts of smoke carried Beaman's soul on it.

Susan pulled up beside an ambulance and we stepped out, covering the rest of the distance on foot. We had barely gotten out of her cruiser when I caught the first familiar whiff of burnt human flesh, and it only grew stronger as we approached the two fire trucks and Melvin's fully marked police truck that were parked in a semi-circle around what was left of Beaman's car.

As we rounded the first fire truck, I saw a young fireman sitting on the back bumper sucking on oxygen. I stopped and looked down at him. The name sewn into the chest of his bunker gear read, *Cole Peterson*. His dark hands were trembling and his big brown eyes were wild. "I've never seen someone burning before," he said to the fire chief who stood over him. "He...his arms looked like burning logs sticking out from his body. And the smell...I never knew a body would smell like that when it burned. I didn't mean to throw up on the scene."

"It's okay, kid," said the fire chief, a forty-something-year-old fellow named Ox Plater. "It happens to all of us."

Ox was a hell of a fire chief and a good mentor. He had fought the fire that took down the police department years ago and his courage under fire—literally—was unmatched.

"What's it look like?" I asked when he turned away from the kid.

"Definitely arson." He removed his helmet and ran a gloved hand across his rough face and through his graying hair. It was hard not to notice the layer of scarred tissue that covered his forehead and both cheeks. He had never volunteered the cause of the scars and I never asked. He shot a thumb toward Melvin, who was photographing the car. "He got here before we did and he said he could smell gasoline. The smoke was dark, so it's possible some motor oil was added to the mixture. There's also glass on the ground around the car—and it's different than the window glass."

I rubbed my chin. "Are you thinking Molotov cocktails?"

"The poor man's grenade." Ox nodded. "It looked to be an amateur job, but somebody really wanted this man dead."

I traded looks with Susan and then thanked Ox. I put my hand on the young fireman's shoulder before walking off. "You'll come out the other side of this day a stronger man and a better firefighter."

He forced a grin, exposing a row of bright teeth, and nodded. "Thank you, sir."

Susan and I then turned away and approached Melvin. I frowned as we walked away from Ox and Cole, remembering the first time I'd smelled burning flesh. It was back when I worked as a young detective in the city of La Mort, and it was my first homicide case. This pervert who had recently gotten out of prison snatched a young girl from a playground and dragged her off into the woods. He'd done unspeakable things to her and then burned her body. I was twenty-two at the time and had already been a detective for two years. Although I'd experienced a lot in four years on the job—two as a patrol cop and two as a general detective—I was not prepared for what I'd seen on that crime scene, and I spent many years wishing I could repay that evil bastard in kind.

I aged quite a bit that night, and it had only gotten worse for me from that point forward. Now, at thirty-three years of age, I was an old soul. Sure, by most standards I was still a young man, but, on the inside, I was old and gray. Maybe a bit wiser, but I was definitely old.

I glanced over at Susan and couldn't help the smile that spread across my face. *And a lot luckier,* I thought.

CHAPTER 4

Susan and I stopped beside Melvin and I studied the car in front of us. Melvin wiped a rivulet of sweat from his shaved head and swatted at a mosquito that landed on his arm. Members of the fire department had set up some flood lights and it lit up the area like daytime, but it also attracted swarms of the Louisiana state bird.

"Want some mosquito repellent?" Susan asked Melvin. He nodded his thanks and she strode off to grab a can of spray from her Tahoe.

While she was gone, I stepped to the front of the car and studied the burn patterns across the shell of the vehicle that was left. It appeared that most of the windows had been busted open. I wasn't sure if the Molotov cocktails had broken the windows or if the arsonist had used some object to break them open before launching his fire bombs into the vehicle.

Although the car had come to rest against the curb at the center of the boulevard, it was obvious by several small piles of glass on the concrete that the initial attack had taken place somewhere between there and a large pickup truck that was parked a dozen yards behind the car. The truck didn't have any burn marks on it, but the front end was damaged and it seemed to match the damage on the back end of the car. There were also several dark burn marks on the concrete to indicate where some of the fuel from the fire grenades had splashed.

I pointed to the blotches along the street. "It looks like the attack began back there and Lance—if, indeed, that is him inside the car— tried to back away, but he slammed into the truck. It seems he then drove forward but got jammed up on the curb. He couldn't have been driving fast while moving forward, otherwise he would've jumped the curb and crashed into the trees. I guess he was burning up pretty bad by that point and writhing in pain. His foot must've come up off the accelerator."

"You said something about *if* it's Lance." Melvin's brow furrowed. "You don't think it's him?"

I looked toward the house, where an older man stood with a small group of people in an arched foyer near the front door. "Did you interview them yet?"

"I interviewed the mansion owner, a Chet Robichaux, and he said he saw Lance get in this car and start it up. He said he returned inside and a few minutes later he thought he heard some kind of explosion. That's when he came outside and saw the car on fire."

"Did he see anyone in the area?"

Melvin wiped his face again, shook his head. "When he saw the car stopped up against the curb, he thought it was some kind of accident. According to him, everyone had already left the event, with the exception of the few people standing there with him now, and they were all inside."

"So, this was a political event?" I dreaded the answer.

"Yep. It was a political meet-and-greet for the citizens of Mechant Loup-North—and most of them support his bid for mayor."

"Does Chet or any of his friends think this is a murder?"

"Not that I know about."

I was thoughtful, then moved closer to the front door so I could look inside and see Lance's body. I reached a hand behind me, toward Melvin. "Can I borrow a flashlight?"

"He was still alive when I arrived." He handed me his light and I flicked it on, aimed the beam of light in what we assumed was Lance's face. We'd have to wait for a formal identification from the coroner's investigation. I noticed that Melvin had turned his head away from the car. "I could hear him moaning. I tried to put the fire out with the extinguisher from my truck, but it was no use. I tried to get inside the car, but the fire was just too hot, you know?"

I detected a hint of pain in Melvin's voice and stopped what I was doing to look into his eyes. "You did everything you could, but there's nothing anyone could've done for him. Even if the fire trucks had arrived with you, they couldn't have saved him. It was already too late."

He nodded slowly. "I appreciate you saying that and I know you're right, but I'm going to question myself for a while, wondering if I could've done something more to save him."

"And that's a good thing, because it means you still care." I slapped his thick shoulder. "When you stop caring is when you need to start worrying."

He grunted. "Okay, Doctor Phil."

I laughed, he didn't, and I turned back to the interior of the car. I'd seen Lance's campaign signs around town and I'd come face-to-face with the man at the Mechant Loup Spring Festival, but the body in front of me looked nothing like him—nor did I expect it to. Fire can do some wicked things to a human body, and it hadn't gone easy on poor Lance. While most burn victims usually die of smoke inhalation before the flames get to them, Lance hadn't been so lucky.

I was pulling my head out of the car when Susan walked up with a can of bug spray. After stepping far away from the car so we wouldn't get repellant on any trace evidence, we took turns carefully wiping a thin layer on our exposed arms and faces. The firemen had stripped off their gear and Ox was directing the cleanup of the area, beginning with the gathering of all of their gear and then the rolling up of the hoses. Once they were done, we began the tedious work of processing the scene.

Other than broken bottle glass and burn marks on the concrete street, there wasn't much to see. After documenting the surrounding area with photographs, sketches, and measurements, we set about documenting the different piles of glass on the concrete and identifying them with evidence markers. While there were different amounts of glass in each pile, they all appeared to have come from the same type of bottles. I knew that some of the bottles had made their way into the car, so that would explain why some of the piles had more glass than the others.

There were only a few shards of window glass on the ground outside of the car and along the street, which confirmed for me that the bottles had been thrown into the vehicle, and not the other way around.

"Do you think we've accounted for all of the bottles?" Susan asked, pointing to the fifth evidence marker on the ground next to the last pile of bottle glass. "I mean, do you think it's possible some of the bottles went completely through the window and none of the pieces fell to the outside?"

I shrugged. "I guess anything's possible, but we know there were at least five different bottles."

She put the unused evidence markers aside and joined me as I peered into the car, trying to get clear photographs of who we believed to be Lance Beaman. It was well into the night and the only light we had now was from the fire trucks. Ox had been nice enough to keep the trucks out there as long as we needed.

"Thank God for these lights," Susan said.

I snapped another picture and nodded, changing positions to get a better angle of his hands and arms. They had folded upward into a pugilistic position, which was common among burn victims. The fire had been so hot it burned the clothes off his body, and his skin was blistered and dark.

Melvin walked up and I could hear him breathing heavily. "I tromped through those trees, up and down the boulevard, and covered the area all around the mansion, but there's no evidence of anyone having been there."

"They could've come and gone by car." I adjusted the zoom, snapped another picture. "What about surveillance cameras? Is this mansion equipped with those?"

"Nope. He said he didn't think anyone had the balls to come back here and try anything, so he never installed any." He raised his hands in defense toward Susan. "Sorry, those were his words, not mine."

Susan waved him off. "You know nothing bothers me."

I was about to snap another picture when Melvin stepped away from us and told someone to stop where they were. I looked up and saw a man approaching from the mansion.

"How much longer will this take?" the man asked. "There are a few guests who haven't left yet and they'd like to go home."

Melvin glanced in my direction, raised an eyebrow.

"Can you find out if they saw anything?" I asked. "If they didn't, show them out of here, but get their contact information. If they did see something, get a statement from them if you don't mind, and I'll follow up with them in the next day or so."

Melvin, who was our Mr. Reliable, nodded and followed Chet to his house. I knew if anyone saw anything, Melvin would get it out of them. He was as solid as they came and fiercely loyal. I was glad to have him on my side.

As I continued photographing the interior of the vehicle, Susan remained in my shadow. After a few minutes, she said, "That's a horrible way to go."

"Yeah, it is, and I'm pretty sure he's in Heaven because he's already gone through hell."

"The smell is horrendous."

I knew she'd smelled dead bodies before, so I didn't have to tell her it would stay with her for a few days—she already knew that much. I began walking toward the back of the car when headlights darted toward us from up North Boulevard.

Ox and his assistant chief got up from where they were sitting on the bumper of the nearest fire truck and approached the vehicle. Ox shielded his eyes and peered into the light. As the vehicle got closer, Ox waved and then turned to call over his shoulder, "Clint, it's the fire marshal, Justin Singleton. Good man and a damn good fire investigator."

CHAPTER 5

Justin Singleton stepped out of a gray older model Crown Victoria and moved to his trunk to retrieve a large box before walking toward the floodlights of the fire trucks. I'd never met him, but if Ox said he was a good man, then that was enough for me.

After shaking Ox's hand and speaking briefly with him and his lieutenant, Justin moved to where Susan and I were standing near the car. He held out his hand and smiled. Although his short cropped hair was frosted, his dark face lit up when he smiled. It made him look ten years younger. "I'm Justin Singleton, and you must be Police Chief Susan Wilson...and Clint Wolf, Chief of Detectives."

"It's just Clint for me."

"And I'm just Susan Wolf." I detected a twinkle in her eye when she said it, and it appeared she'd been waiting for an opportunity to use her new name.

Justin apologized, but Susan waved him off. Placing the large box on the ground beside us, Justin turned to the scene and took it all in for a moment before moving closer. He surveyed the evidence markers, using his flashlight and squatting low to get a closer look at each pile of glass, then moved toward the truck and examined the damage to the front of it. He then strode toward where the car had come to rest and slowly moved his light over every inch of its surface, starting with the hood and working his way along the sides and toward the trunk.

"Did y'all document the scene already?"

"Yeah, we've got photographs, sketches, and measurements. I'll make copies of everything for you." I pointed toward the piles of glass. "We didn't touch any of the evidence, though, because we were waiting for you to get here."

He rubbed his face and shook his head. "This was a brutal attack, but a clumsy one. Whoever did this probably learned how to make Molotov cocktails watching some online video. They're lucky they didn't set themselves on fire." He shook his head. "The Internet is a dangerous thing, that's for sure."

"What do you think they used?" I asked. "Melvin thought he smelled gasoline."

"They definitely used gasoline—and motor oil—and they corked the bottles with rags." He bent and pointed to the remnants of some fabric near the broken neck of one of the bottles that had bounced off of the car when it had been thrown. He straightened. "They deployed at least five fire bombs—could've been six if one of the bottles went completely into the car—and they did it in a hurry. It looks very rushed and unorganized, almost angry."

"Have you worked this kind of case before?" I asked. "Personally, I've worked arson murders, but nothing like this."

"Like you, I've worked arson murders, but they mostly consisted of a husband or wife dousing their spouse with gasoline and then tossing them a lighter." Justin walked to his box and removed some metal paint cans and strung a camera over his neck. "I'll recover some samples and send them to the lab to confirm the mixture, but I can already smell what it is." He grinned and his face lit up again. "My nose can actually detect what brand of oil was used in the mixture, and if the gasoline was ten percent ethanol or ethanol free."

"Really?" Melvin asked, walking up from behind us carrying some type of ledger.

"No," Justin said. "I was only kidding."

We laughed and I walked over to Melvin while Justin began collecting the shards of glass and packaging them in separate cans. "What do you have there?" I asked, pointing toward his hands.

Melvin hefted the ledger. "This is a sign-in sheet for the guests who attended the political event Lance had out here tonight. The name of every person who attended is listed here, along with their addresses, phone numbers, and email addresses."

"Really?" I stared blankly at the ledger. "Why on earth would they collect all of that information? And how lucky is that for us?"

"Well, turns out, it's not luck at all—it's actually common practice." He flipped open the ledger and turned it so I could see the list of names and accompanying information. "Whenever they have one of these political functions, they gather up all of this information so they can harass these people later and make sure they go out and vote on election day. They also contact them for more money or to put signs in their yards or to try and get them to volunteer for different things."

"Huh." I grunted. "That's smart."

Melvin nodded and pushed out his chest. "Thanks, I thought so myself."

I took the ledger from him and thanked him for his help. It was already way past midnight, so he said he'd better go check on the rest of the town. He started to walk away, but stopped and turned toward Susan and me. "It's damn good to have y'all back."

I thought about the cold waterfall in Jamaica, the bumpy Jeep ride to the town of Hell, Grand Caymans, and the beach buggy ride to the private pristine beach in Cozumel, and frowned. "It's not good to be back."

His face dropped and his shoulders drooped, looking genuinely offended, but then I smiled and told him I was only joking. He seemed to cheer up a little. As we watched him walk to his truck and drive away, Susan nudged me with her shoulder and whispered, "You weren't joking at all—not one bit."

"I love this town and I love my job," I said, "but damn, that was a great honeymoon."

"Yeah, I could sure get used to lazing around with you all day and then going to dinner at night."

"Maybe when we get old and gray…"

She shined her flashlight up at my dark brown hair, pointed to what I was sure was a white hair. "You mean, like, tomorrow?"

I was about to argue when I heard the distant roar of an engine, and it sounded like it was coming from the front of the street.

"Heads up," Ox called from the fire truck, "someone's coming in hot."

I hurried to Susan's Tahoe and tossed the ledger inside, then stood in the middle of the street shining a light toward the approaching vehicle. The headlights were on bright and the yellow flashers were blinking. Whoever was driving was swerving from side to side, as though trying to keep the car under control. I felt a presence beside me and heard Susan's voice tell me to get out of the road.

I continued shining my light in the area of the windshield as the car drew nearer. "They'd better stop, or I'm going to draw down on them."

"You're going to have to…" I heard Susan's gun clear her holster and I did the same as the car smashed through the yellow crime scene tape that we had strung up earlier. Susan and I both sidestepped toward the edge of the boulevard. I held my breath as the car rapidly approached, waiting for it to crash into the back of Susan's cruiser. To my surprise, the driver smashed the brakes and jerked the wheel to the right. The car skidded to a lurching stop at a sharp angle several feet from Susan's vehicle.

I could see a shadowy figure in the front seat and knew it represented the driver, but I couldn't tell much more than that, because the window was tinted. The driver seemed to be alone and was moving around a bit. Finally, the driver door flung open, but then everything went still for a long moment. The only sound we heard was the humming of the car's engine and the only smell we detected was that of Lance's burnt carcass.

"Driver, I need you to step out of the car and keep your hands where I can see them." Keeping my pistol at my side, I aimed the flashlight above the door frame and took a step forward, waiting for the driver to reveal himself. "You've driven through a crime scene barrier and I need you to identify yourself and demonstrate that you're unarmed."

In my peripheral vision, I could see Susan's shadow fanning out to my right. She was circling around to the back of the vehicle so she and I could triangulate our gunfire on the driver if it came to that.

"Driver," I said, moving in Susan's direction and trying to get my light around the edge of the door, "I need you to show me your hands!"

Still no movement from the car.

"Susan, can you see anything?" I whispered out the corner of my mouth, trying to force my voice to carry only in her direction. She was still about twenty feet away from the car, but she had made her way to the back corner area and should be able to have a visual on the interior of the cab.

"I'm lighting it up," Susan said, and I heard her flashlight slide from its holder. In the next instant, the bright beam from her flashlight reached out through the darkness and lit up the cab. I still couldn't see anything, but I heard Susan gasp. "Clint, it's a woman...and she's crying!"

CHAPTER 6

"Covering," Susan said in a soft but firm voice, letting me know she would keep her pistol trained on the woman until I made contact and ensured she wasn't a threat.

After scanning our surroundings and turning my ear to the wind to make sure her actions hadn't been meant to distract us from something else, I turned my light off and moved quietly forward through the shadows. When I was about ten feet from the open door I could hear soft sobs coming from the driver's seat. I turned toward the wreckage and noticed the woman had a perfect view of Lance's car between the fire trucks.

I didn't recognize the woman, but I immediately realized she must've recognized Lance's car. I holstered my pistol and reached out to open the door. The woman didn't even look up as I did so. Her face was buried in her hands and she was bawling. I could see tiny twinkles of light as her tears fell through the beam of Susan's flashlight and to the ground.

The woman wore a long dress that was multi-colored and had a smattering of shapes printed all over it. She was in her mid-fifties, from what I could tell of her hair color, and stout. A ring that looked two sizes too small was stretched over her left ring finger, and there was a giant diamond attached to it. For a split second I wondered if the diamond on the ring I'd bought for Susan was large enough, but then I quickly dismissed the thought and turned my attention to the woman.

"Ma'am, are you okay?" As soon as the words left my mouth, I gave myself a mental kick in the ass. *Of course she's not okay, Clint!* I reached out and gently touched her shoulder. I identified myself but the woman didn't even move her hands from her face. As far as she was concerned, she was alone there in the car, grief-stricken and utterly helpless.

Over my shoulder, I heard Susan calling in the license plate. I spoke to the woman again, but she still didn't respond. It didn't take long for Beth to radio Susan and tell her the car belonged to Nicole Beaman. My heart sank. *How in the hell did she find out about this?*

"Mrs. Beaman," I said, "can you look at me?"

The woman didn't budge.

I glanced over at Susan and she indicated with her head for me to back away. When I did, she moved in and dropped beside the woman. She leaned close and began speaking softly into the woman's ear. I couldn't hear what was being said, but it didn't take long for Mrs. Beaman to slowly remove her hands from her face and turn to look at Susan. Although she was staring directly at Susan, it appeared from my vantage point that she was looking straight through my wife, unseeing.

"Ma'am, what are you doing here?" Susan asked in a coaxing voice. "How did you know to come over?"

Her chin trembling uncontrollably, Mrs. Beaman said, "I...it was Peggy...my friend, Peggy. Peggy Robichaux called me to say there had been an accident. She said...she told me there had been a fire and...and she told me Lance had...that Lance was...oh, God! It's true, isn't it?" She pointed past Susan to the shell of a car. "Is Lance inside of his car? I wanted to go see for myself, but...oh, dear, I just can't bring myself to walk over there. Please, you've got to tell me...is that Lance?"

Susan frowned and lowered her head. "Ma'am, I'm so sorry to have to be the one to tell you this, but it's true...someone did this to your husband."

Mrs. Beaman let out a shrill cry that must have disturbed half the people in the town's cemetery. She fell out of the car and collapsed into Susan's chest. Susan planted her right knee on the ground and caught her before she could face-plant into the hard concrete. I rushed forward and helped Susan roll Mrs. Beaman onto her back. We placed her gently onto the ground, extended her legs, and placed her arms directly at her sides. I turned when a dark shadow fell over us. It was Ox.

"I've already called for an ambulance," he said, his face showing concern.

I nodded and Susan and I backed away so Ox and his lieutenant could assess Mrs. Beaman's condition. A few minutes later, Justin joined us and told me he had everything he needed.

"The evidence for arson is insurmountable; I found five discernible points of origin, the use of an accelerant is obvious and will be confirmed through lab results, and the fire burned hotter than hell in summer. I know we've never worked together before, but I'm guessing it's like everywhere—I'll handle the arson aspect and you'll handle the murder?"

"Yeah, sounds good."

Justin pursed his lips as he stared down at Lance's wife. "It's a good thing she stopped back here. Had she seen her husband in that condition…" He paused and shook his head. "They'd be burying her right along side of him."

Ox and his lieutenant had revived Mrs. Beaman and they were speaking softly with her, letting her know everything was going to be okay and that an ambulance was en route. I was hoping the ambulance would arrive soon and take her away before the coroner's investigator showed up for Lance's body.

"Clint, look over there."

I turned to see where Susan was pointing. At the beginning of the wide driveway, up near the house, a man was standing and watching the scene. He was staring toward Lance's car and I didn't think he knew we were back by Susan's Tahoe.

"Is that the homeowner?" I asked, squinting against the floodlights that stood between us and the house.

"I think so. He's been there for a few minutes. I saw a splash of light when the front door opened. He walked to the edge of the driveway and just stopped and stared."

"I'm going talk to him." I walked off and Justin stepped in behind me while Susan waited with Ox and the others. When I walked past Lance's car and approached the man, he gave a solemn nod of his head.

"Clint, nice to see you again."

I knew the man from around town, but we'd never been formally introduced. I shook his hand and introduced him to Justin.

"Mr. Robichaux, can I ask you a few questions?" I began. "I know it's late, but since you're already out here…"

"Sure, that's why I walked over. I've got some information."

"What is it?" I was curious, but didn't show it.

"Well, Officer Saltzman confiscated the ledger, but there was one man whose name isn't on it, and I think he might know something."

I cocked my head to the side. "Who is this man and why isn't his name on the ledger?"

"No one knows who he is. Lance noticed him first and asked me about him, but I didn't know who he was talking about at first. He said the man didn't look like a supporter."

"Go on," I said.

"Well, most of the people at the meet-and-greet were familiar to someone in our group, but none of us knew this man. When he arrived, he acted like he was supporting Lance—he even let my wife put a sticker on his shirt—but now I think he might be involved."

"How do you know he didn't sign the ledger?" I asked.

"My wife and daughter were taking names at the door and getting everyone to sign the ledger. When he walked in, he said he didn't feel comfortable giving out his personal information. He said he'd had his identity stolen before, so my wife didn't press the issue and she didn't think anything of it. That is, until a minute ago when I told her Officer Saltzman had taken the ledger."

"You said none of y'all knew this man. How do you know?"

"I just called everyone who attended and asked if any of them had seen him before or if they spoke with him during the night. Those who remembered him said they didn't know his name or anything about him."

I wondered how Chet was able to call everyone who had been at the party when his ledger was locked in Susan's cruiser. He must've seen the look on my face, because he held up his phone. "I took screenshots of the pages before giving the ledger to your officer."

Slick bastard, I thought, making a note to keep an eye on him. "While you're here, I might as well cover the basics with you." I pulled out my notepad. "You called nine-one-one and reported an accident. Is that correct?"

He nodded. "At first, I thought it was a wreck. I saw Lance's car on fire and it was stopped up against the curb. I also noticed the damage to my son's car, so I thought maybe he'd backed up and hit the truck, then sped forward and crashed into the curb. Since the gas tank is in the rear of the car, I thought maybe that's how the fire had started, but I couldn't be sure. When I saw the way Officer Saltzman was acting and when I heard him call for reinforcements, I knew there was probably foul play involved."

"What first drew your attention to the car?"

"I had walked Lance outside and watched him get into his car. I had just gone back inside and was still entertaining a few guests when I heard some kind of explosion." He scowled. "It didn't sound like a bomb, or anything impressive like that, but it was loud enough to make me take notice. That's when I opened the door and saw all the fire and smoke."

"Did you see anyone in the area? Anyone at all?"

"No, Detective. I didn't see anyone. Like I told Officer Saltzman, it all happened so fast that I didn't even have time to think. All of my attention was on Lance's car. I was running toward it to try and get him out, but when I got close I knew it was too late. The fire was too hot and I couldn't—"

Chet stopped talking for a second and lowered his head, squeezing back tears. After a few long moments, he continued, but his voice was lower and strained. "I couldn't get to my friend and help him. I tried to reach for the door to open it, but the flames were too big. There was just no use. No matter how hard I tried, I couldn't help him. When Officer Saltzman arrived, he did everything he could to get to Lance. He risked his life, he really did. We had all backed up in case the car exploded, but Officer Saltzman wasn't bothered by that possibility. He tried to put out the blaze with his fire extinguisher and then he kept trying to reach through the window to grab Lance. He really went above and beyond what was expected."

Chet sighed deeply. "He's a hero. He did the best he could to help a total stranger, with no regard for his own safety."

My chest swelled with pride hearing the way Chet spoke about Melvin. Of course, he wasn't telling me anything I didn't already know. Having worked with Melvin as long as I had, I already knew he was a courageous officer who would put his life on the line for his community, and he was as loyal as they came.

"Would I be correct in assuming you and Lance Beaman were really close?" I asked slowly.

"We were."

"Do you know of anyone who might want him dead? Problems with anyone? Bad business deals? Any enemies?"

Chet took a deep breath and exhaled. "There is one person I know who might want him dead...who would benefit from his death."

"Who's that?" I asked, not sure if I wanted to know the answer.

"You already know."

I noticed Justin cock his head to the side.

"Do I?"

"You do." He fixed me with a hard stare as he nodded. "Everyone knows the one person who stands to gain the most through Lance's death is your boss."

"Who's your boss?" Justin asked.

CHAPTER 7

It was no easy task getting Lance Beaman's body out of the car. The coroner's investigator had arrived around four in the morning and it took about an hour for us to remove the body, visually examine it, and force it into the bag. The only part of the body not touched by fire was the seat of his pants, and we found a wallet containing four hundred and thirty-two dollars, several receipts, three credit cards in Lance Beaman's name, and Lance's driver's license.

My mind raced the entire time we worked. I knew Pauline Cain. I was certain she was not capable of murder, but I couldn't let my relationship with her cloud my judgment. Of course, even if it did, there was Justin, and he had no ties to Pauline or anyone else in our small town. And while Justin didn't answer to Pauline, I did, and I had to protect myself in case she got offended when I asked for her alibi. I was, after all, an at-will employee and she could fire me for any reason—and accusing her of murder might be as good a reason as any.

Once we were done examining the body and the coroner's investigator had left with it, Justin and I exchanged business cards and he told me he'd be back in touch soon. He then loaded up his metal evidence cans, packed up his gear, and drove off.

"What's next?" Susan asked as we watched Justin drive away. Ox and his lieutenant had already packed up their lights and were fixing to leave the scene.

I surveyed the scene, making sure we'd picked up all of our gear and not left any evidentiary stone unturned. As brutal as the crime had been, there wasn't much to the scene. Someone had firebombed the hell out of Lance Beaman's car and then disappeared. Once the autopsy confirmed it was Lance, then we'd have at least two suspects.

The one with the most to gain, as Chet Robichaux had pointed out, was Pauline. The other was Zack Pitre, who was the third candidate in the race for Mechant Loup's mayor. Of course, Zack was virtually unknown, had raised no money, and, thanks to his horrible performance at the one debate they'd had, some were betting he wouldn't even place third in the race.

I shared my thoughts with Susan and she nodded.

"Yeah," she said, smirking, "even if Zack did kill Lance, he wouldn't stand a chance in hell of getting the job. He'd have to kill—" Her mouth suddenly clamped shut. "Oh, shit! What if it is him and he's going after Pauline next?"

We didn't waste any time getting out of there. We caught up with the fire trucks in seconds and sped past them on North Boulevard, heading straight for another mansion—this one owned by Pauline.

When her husband had been alive, Pauline and Hays had owned a chain of restaurants across the south. They had been one of—if not *the*—wealthiest couples in town. After Hays had been killed and Pauline had taken stock of her life, she'd sold off all of her restaurants except the one in town and had thrown herself into local politics. She'd donated a lot of her wealth to the various organizations within town and she'd even helped me with a tough situation some time back. I owed her big time, and I felt bad about the questions I might have to ask her. That is, if she was still alive. If Zack would have any chance at all of being our town's next mayor, then both Pauline and Lance would have to be out of the way.

I grabbed the "oh shit" bar above my head and held on as Susan turned the corner and raced south toward the Mechant Loup Bridge. We nearly went airborne at the top of the bridge. When we settled to the other side, the Tahoe jostled roughly, rattling my teeth. I knew better than to complain, because that would only make Susan drive faster.

Buildings blurred by and it wasn't long before I had to hold onto the handle again as Susan turned onto the right street. Pauline still lived in her family mansion at the end of Kate Drive.

It was surrounded by dozens of acres of pristine land. Large palm trees and lampposts lined both sides of the mostly bare street, and the lampposts lit up the early morning darkness like it was the middle of a bright day. The end of the street opened into a large cul-de-sac that boasted an enormous waterfall at its center. I'd always thought the mansion looked out of place in the quaint little town of Mechant

Loup, but it seemed the new residents of Mechant Loup-North were determined to make that type of house the norm, rather than the exception.

"Look," Susan said, pointing, "her gate's open. Doesn't she usually keep it closed?"

"Not anymore." I explained that she had grown tired of answering the buzzer and opening the gate. When her husband was alive, they had an assistant named Stephen Butler who would man the gate, but Pauline had decided to retire him because she didn't think it was appropriate having a man living in the house now that she was a widow.

Susan cruised through the double gates and up the cobblestone driveway to the front of the mansion, where I jumped out before she could put her cruiser in *park*. I sprinted up the flight of stone steps and banged on the large wooden door while also ringing the doorbell like a madman.

"Come on," I said under my breath. "Answer the door."

Susan was already out of the Tahoe and began making her way around toward the back of the house when I saw the knob turn.

"Sue, the door's opening..." I stepped back and waited as the heavy door slowly creaked open. When it was wide enough for me to see inside, I saw Pauline standing there in a terrycloth robe, her black hair a tangled mess and her eyes squinting. Never afraid to show off her physical assets, the robe was parted down the front and a healthy amount of cleavage was exposed through the top of an old faded Lynyrd Skynyrd tank top. I averted my eyes.

"Ma'am, is everything okay?"

"What in God's name is going on, Clint? It's barely five in the morning. Why are you even here? I thought you were still on your honeymoon." She leaned out and looked past me. I saw her eyes widen and knew she must've seen Susan with her gun drawn. Only then did she pull the front of her robe closed, but I think it was her subconscious way of protecting herself from danger. "Why does she have her gun out?"

I glanced at Susan, who indicated toward the back of the house with her head. "I'll do a quick security check."

"Clint, what on earth is going on?"

"Let's get you inside and I'll explain." I followed Pauline into the house and glanced around the foyer. Nothing seemed out of place and I was relieved to note there were no gasoline cans, quarts of oil, or other supplies for making Molotov cocktails. I quickly moved across the house and made my way to the back door, opening it just as Susan rounded the corner. "Anything?"

She shook her head. "All's clear."

Susan followed me back to the living room, where we found Pauline standing with her arms wrapped around the front of her torso. "Will one of you tell me what's going on?"

"You might be in danger." I studied her face, trying to detect any hint that she already knew why we were there. I saw nothing but a slight look of horror.

"Danger?" She glanced at Susan and then back at me. "From who? Why?"

"Someone murdered Lance Beaman tonight. Set his car on fire and burned him to—"

"Oh, no!"

CHAPTER 8

Susan was quicker than me—that wasn't surprising, considering she was a mixed martial arts champion—and she caught Pauline before her head hit the floor. The robe fell open and Susan did her best to keep her decent.

"Go see if you can find some fruit juice in the kitchen," Susan ordered, stretching Pauline out on her back and snatching a pillow from the sofa to tuck under her legs.

I hurried to the kitchen and stared wildly about. The place was immaculate and the wooden cabinets looked as though they'd been hand-carved out of a single piece of wood. I began jerking cabinet doors open, searching frantically for a glass, but I couldn't seem to find one.

Finally, I spotted a glass on the table in the neighboring dining room. After rushing over and snatching it from the table, I tried to find the refrigerator. I pulled open the larger cabinet doors, thinking maybe the refrigerator was hiding in one of them. When I felt I'd taken too long, I rushed to the sink and filled the glass with water from a spigot that was probably made of solid gold. I then took it to the living room.

Pauline was alert, but appeared confused, and Susan was cradling her head in her lap. The robe was loose, so I kept my head turned and handed Susan the glass.

"This is some strange-looking fruit juice," she mumbled.

"I couldn't find the refrigerator."

It was obvious by the trembling of her shoulders that Susan was trying really hard not to laugh as she carefully poured a swallow of water into Pauline's mouth.

"Take a little sip," Susan said. "You'll be fine. I can call an ambulance for you, if you like."

"No, please don't," Pauline said. "This happens when I'm overcome with emotion."

I cursed silently. She had fainted when I notified her of her husband's death, so I should've expected the same reaction. While Susan took her time with Pauline, I excused myself and walked outside. The sun was starting to rise. It wasn't daylight yet, but I could see that the shadows on the outer edges of the property were starting to get scared away by a faint glow in the eastern sky.

I pulled out my cell phone and called Beth at the office. She picked up and immediately asked if everything was okay. "Is Mayor Pauline in danger?"

"Everything's fine out here. What's Melvin up to?"

"He's right here finishing up a report. Want to talk to him?"

"Yes, please." When Melvin got on the phone, I asked if he knew where Zack Pitre lived.

"Hold up, I'll have Beth run it." After a few moments of speaking with Beth in the background, Melvin got back on the phone. I could hear papers shuffling. "According to this, he stays off of Cypress Highway on the east side."

"Before you knock off, can you take a drive to his place to see if he's home?"

"Sure, what's up?"

I told him what Chet had said about Pauline and our thoughts about the possibility of Zack taking out all of the competition. "Pauline seemed genuinely shocked to find out about Lance. Hell, she fainted like she did when I told her about her husband, and we know she had nothing to do with that, but we do have to keep an open mind."

"I see Chet's point about Mayor Cain having the most to gain by Lance's murder, but I can't see her committing a murder just to keep her job."

"I can't either, but people have been killed for less, and usually the people closest to the killer are the ones who are shocked the most by their actions."

"I guess so." Melvin sighed. "I'll head out to Zack's place and see what I can find out."

"Who's coming on dayshift?" I asked.

"Baylor Rice."

Susan had hired Baylor almost two years ago, increasing her number of officers to four. She was then able to run twelve-hour shifts, with at least one officer covering the town at all times. Melvin and Amy Cooke, her most seasoned officers, worked the night shift while Baylor and Takecia Gayle worked the day shift. Originally from a small town in North Carolina called Sylva, Baylor had found his way to Mechant Loup after doing a four-year stint in the military, and I was glad he'd made it down here. He was a good kid and a quick study.

"Why don't you get Baylor to head that way with you? Just in case."

"Gotcha."

"Oh, and approach him under the pretext that he's a victim. He'll give you more information if he thinks we're there to help him."

"Will do."

I ended the call and was about to walk inside when I heard a car approaching. I shoved my phone in my pocket and dropped my hand next to my pistol. The car slowed as it drove through the open gates and I was about to draw my pistol when Susan called from the doorway behind me.

"It's okay, Clint. Pauline called a friend to stay with her."

I relaxed and watched as the woman parked in front of the house and exited the car, purse tucked under her arm and baseball cap shoved deep on her head. I didn't recognize her. After exchanging pleasantries with Susan, the woman disappeared inside and Susan joined me on the cobblestone drive.

"You know, we'll have to question her about her whereabouts soon," I said, staring up at the house.

"When do you plan on doing that?"

"Just as soon as I talk to Sheriff Turner."

"Sheriff Turner?" There was a quizzical expression on Susan's face. "Why?"

"Insurance."

CHAPTER 9

Melvin Saltzman turned in his report, walked to his office, and closed the door. He pulled out his cell phone, called his wife. "Hey, Claire," he said to her voicemail. "I guess you're in the shower. I'm going to be home a little late. I have to check out something. Do you think you can wait a little before going in to work? Well, I guess I'd better go now. Please kiss Delilah for me."

After hesitating for a second, he ended the call. Delilah was going to be three in August, and Claire had recently decided to go back to work at the bank. When she first got pregnant, Claire vowed to be a stay-at-home mom and Melvin had supported her decision. He didn't make a killing at the police department, but the bills were getting paid and they had a little extra for a night out here and there. When Claire started talking about taking Delilah to Disney World earlier in the year, they had both sat down and crunched the numbers.

"Either you have to go back to school and get a law degree, or I've got to go back to work," Claire had said that night in January. "At this rate, we'll never be able to take our daughter on a family vacation, we'll never be able to get a new car, we'll be dead before the house is paid off, and we still haven't paid all the doctor bills from Delilah being—"

"I get your point." Melvin didn't like feeling as though he couldn't give his wife the life she wanted. He had always wanted to be a lawyer, but there was no way he could take a break from working to pursue that dream, and they definitely couldn't afford to pile hefty student loans on top of a house mortgage and a car note.

He and Claire had been high school sweethearts and they had gotten married soon after graduation. Neither of them wanted to live with their parents, so they each went to work—Melvin for the police department and Claire for a bank in Central Chateau Parish.

When Claire got pregnant, she began talking about how nice it would be to stay home and raise their children. Melvin had assured her she would be able to do it, but that was before Claire started talking about Disney World. "I'll get a second job. Maybe I can run some swamp tours or something."

"Your first job is demanding enough." Claire had frowned and shook her head. "No, I'm going back to the bank. I spoke with my old manager last week and he said they have an opening. I can start anytime I want."

Melvin had felt betrayed. He told Claire everything and got her input on every major decision he made, yet she had decided to go back to work on her own, without even letting him know what she was thinking. She told him he was being foolish when he brought it up, so he dropped it.

Now, staring down at his phone, he wondered how she would take the news that he was working late.

"Hey, Melvin, are you ready?"

Melvin jerked around to see Baylor's head sticking inside the door to his office.

"Sorry if I interrupted something," Baylor explained. "I knocked three times really hard, and Beth told me it would be okay to just open the door."

Melvin straightened and waved it off. "Yeah, of course, no problem. Let's go find this guy."

Melvin led the way to the parking lot below and they climbed into his truck. As they drove toward the little bridge that separated the western side of the town from the eastern side, Melvin explained what all had happened the night before and why they were making contact with Zack Pitre.

"At this point, we don't know if he's a suspect or a potential victim, so we need to be careful how we approach him. We can't go in with guns blazing, but we have to be careful in case he is the killer."

Baylor's face was twisted in a weird expression and Melvin asked him what was wrong.

"It's just that, um, one of my good buddies—the one who told me about this place—died in a helicopter crash during a military training exercise in California." Baylor paused and wiped his face. "He would've survived, but he was trapped in the harness and…and, um…he burned to death."

"Wow, I'm so sorry to hear that." Melvin frowned as he read the hurt on Baylor's face. "If you ever need to talk about it, I'm here."

Baylor nodded. "Thanks. The worst part about it though? The pilot escaped without a scratch. Instead of running into the fire to try and save my friend, he ran away from the helicopter because he was afraid it would explode."

Melvin gripped the steering wheel and looked straight ahead as he remembered how he had tried to rescue Lance the night before. His hands still burned in places from where the flames had licked him with their unforgiving tongues. Each time the throbbing pain returned he simply accepted it, knowing it was nothing compared to the horror that Lance had endured during his last minutes on earth. Sure, Melvin had been terrified. He thought the fuel tank would explode and the flames would swallow him up just as they were swallowing up Lance, but he couldn't just stand idly by and watch while the man was tortured.

"Did you see it?" Baylor's voice broke through Melvin's thoughts.

"See what?"

"The man burning?"

Melvin sighed, nodded slowly. "I tried to help him, but I couldn't. The vehicle was already engulfed and I just couldn't get to him."

Baylor pointed to the back of Melvin's right hand, where a blister had formed earlier in the morning. "Is that from your efforts?"

Melvin just kept driving.

Baylor pointed out several more blisters and a portion of Melvin's short sleeved uniform shirt that was melted. "If that damn pilot would've had a small fraction of the injuries on his body that you have, I would've felt differently."

In his peripheral vision, Melvin saw Baylor turn his head to stare out the passenger side window, and it looked like he took a swipe at his eyes with his right hand. After a few moments of silence, Baylor asked, "Did you know this man? This Lance Beaman—is he your friend or something?"

Melvin shook his head. "I don't even like him. He was an asshole and if he would've won the election for mayor, he would've gotten rid of Susan and Clint, so there's no way in hell I was ever going to work for him."

"You see what I mean!" Baylor slapped the dashboard. "You

risked your life for an asshole, but that damn pilot couldn't risk his life for a brother in arms—someone who covered his ass while he did the flying."

Melvin only nodded. He was through talking about it, and he certainly didn't want to think about it anymore. Each time he did, his heart started racing and he'd have trouble breathing. At the time, he didn't think of anything but getting Lance out of that car. In the hours since then, all he could think about was his family.

What would have happened to Claire and Delilah had he died in that blaze alongside Lance? There was no way Claire would have been able to support herself and a baby on her salary alone. She made less than half of what he made, so she would never have been able to pay all of the bills. Hell, she couldn't even pay the house note and still be able to buy food for them.

Melvin tried to push the thoughts from his mind as they approached Zack's house from the north. He squinted to read the house number on the gray mailbox they were approaching and nodded. "This is it."

Baylor grunted. "Not what I'd expect from a politician. I thought they all had money."

Melvin had been around local politics long enough to know better, but he was also a little surprised by the house. It was a small white house with wooden siding that had seen its better days many years ago. Most of the paint was chipped away, exposing bare wood beneath. The green shutters were nonfunctional and most of them were rotten, with one of them hanging precariously from a single hinge and threatening to fall to the ground. The tin roof was mostly orange from rust. Melvin didn't suspect the place had central air and heating, because there were two window units on the northern side of the house.

"I guess he fired the yard boy," Baylor said as Melvin pulled to a stop behind a small gray SUV that was parked under a narrow carport. The grass hadn't been cut in at least a few weeks and thick patches of clovers gave the yard a bumpy appearance. "It's a lazy man who won't keep up his yard."

Melvin shut off the engine and stepped out of his truck. "Maybe he's been too busy campaigning to cut the grass."

"Or too busy burning people."

The comment made Melvin track his hand toward his weapon. He stepped forward and felt the front quarter panel on the gray SUV. It was cold, but that didn't mean anything. The murder had taken place many hours earlier.

Melvin approached the front of the house and motioned for Baylor to step to one side of the door while he stepped to the opposite side. He knocked loudly. The sun was climbing to the east, but the dew hadn't burned off the grass yet and they'd tracked moisture on the concrete. Melvin noticed theirs were the only wet shoeprints on the walkway. He knocked again.

"I'm coming, I'm coming," cackled a woman's voice from inside. "Hold your damn horses!"

Footsteps pounded toward the door and it finally jerked open. On the other side of the screen door, a short robust woman wearing a thin nightgown stood staring up at them. Her eyes bore into Melvin first, then Baylor. "What is this?"

"We're sorry to disturb you, ma'am," Melvin began, "but we really need to speak with your husband, Zack Pitre."

"Well, that won't be possible." The woman slammed the door shut and Melvin heard her footsteps moving deeper into the house.

"What the hell?" Melvin had asked Beth to run an address inquiry and she gave him this address. He banged on the door again. The woman began cursing from inside. She tramped back to the door and flung it open.

"What now?"

"I apologize, ma'am, but I was under the impression that Zack Pitre lived here."

"He did...before he died."

Melvin's brow furrowed. "Died? When?"

"About ten years ago."

"Oh, I'm sorry," Melvin said, thinking quickly. "I must be looking for Junior then."

The woman grunted, turned her back on the officers. "Zack! Some people are here for you!"

Melvin heard rustling from a back bedroom and, in a groggy voice, someone called out, "Is it about the election?"

"How the hell should I know?" the woman retorted.

Melvin tried to see inside the house, but it was too dark. Bumping sounds came from a hidden room to the left. He glanced at Baylor. "Anything?"

Baylor shook his head. "It's too dark."

Finally, a door slammed and a young man walked up shrugging into an oversized shirt. When he pulled it down over the white belly that hung over his beltline, he righted the thick glasses on his nose and pushed open the screen door.

"Can I help—oh, cops." He took a step back into the house. "My mom didn't say y'all were cops. What's going on?"

"We're here on a welfare check," Melvin explained.

Zack looked confused. "I don't know what you mean. What's a welfare check?"

"We're here to make sure you're okay."

"I'm fine." He looked over at Baylor and then back at Melvin. "Is that all?"

"Well, there's been an incident and we believe your life might be in danger." Melvin took a deep breath and exhaled slowly, allowing Zack to process what he'd said. When Zack only stared blankly at him, Melvin continued. "One of the mayoral candidates has been killed—murdered—and we want to make sure no one is targeting—"

"Which one?" Zack's face actually lit up and Melvin almost slapped him. "Was it Pauline Cain?"

"No, it was Lance Beaman."

Melvin found the grin on Zack's face disturbing.

"So, does that mean I'm number two in the polls now?" Zack asked.

Trying his best to maintain his calm, Melvin said, "A man was brutally murdered and all you care about are the poll numbers?"

"I mean, I feel sorry for him, but there's nothing I can do about that now. I have a campaign to run."

"Do you mind telling me where you were last night?"

"Sure. I was here at home with my mom."

"And I guess she'll be willing to verify that?"

"You damn right I'll verify that," called the woman from the back of the house. "He was here with me all night. He didn't kill nobody. My Zachary wouldn't hurt a fly if it landed in his cereal."

Melvin's phone began to ring. He pulled it from his pocket and glanced at the screen. *Claire.* Ignoring the call, he told Zack to contact the police department if he saw anything suspicious. "I don't want to alarm you, but until we know what's going on, it's best if you take some precautions."

Zack smiled and ushered them to the door. "I'll be just fine, officer—what'd you say your name was again?"

"Melvin. Melvin Saltzman."

"I'll be just fine, Officer Melvin."

"What do you think?" Baylor asked when they got in Melvin's truck. "He's acting a little weird. Do you think it's because he's guilty or is he just a few slices shy of a loaf of bread?"

"He doesn't seem to be bothered by the news, that's for sure." Melvin's phone started ringing again. There seemed to be something about the tone of the ring that made him think Claire was angry.

Baylor indicated toward the phone with his head. "Maybe you should take that."

"Yeah…maybe."

CHAPTER 10

Sheriff Buck Turner's Ranch

It was a little before eight o'clock when I turned onto the long dirt road that led to Sheriff Turner's barn. Susan had asked several times why we were meeting with the sheriff, but I kept giving her the same answer: *insurance.*

I had called his cell and asked for a meeting at his office, but he told me he'd taken the day off and that I could meet him at his ranch. I'd never been there before, so he'd given me the directions.

"If by *insurance* you mean we're milking cows," Susan said as the barn came into view through the trees up ahead, "you're on your own."

I only smiled and parked near a metal gate. We hadn't even stepped out of my Tahoe when Sheriff Turner came galloping up on a large brown horse. At six-foot-three and two-hundred-forty pounds, he was a big man, but the horse made him look like a giant. That— and his worn leather boots, large Stetson, and the single-action 1875 Outlaw Colt .45 revolver riding low on his hip—gave the appearance that he'd just stepped out of a Louis L'Amour novel. Like the sheriffs of the Old West, he was tough as nails and as loyal a friend as anyone could hope to have. He'd always been there when we needed him, and I was hoping he'd be there once more.

"Howdy, Clint." Sheriff Turner dropped from the horse with deceptive grace. He had worked cows his entire life, until a few years ago when he decided to jump into politics and run for the top law enforcement job in the parish. With absolutely no political experience to his name, he'd unseated the most popular sheriff in

Louisiana. He was now two years into his first four-year term. "It looks like Pauline's chances of keeping her job just went up to about ninety-nine percent."

I walked to the gate and waited for him to open it. "That's why I'm here."

He removed his Stetson and pulled a rag from his back pocket, wiped his face dry. Although it was still early in the morning, it was already seventy degrees and it promised to be a hot one. "Please don't tell me she's involved with killing off her competition."

I raised a hand. "I have no evidence whatsoever and I don't think it's in her character to do something like that, but I've got to protect myself and the integrity of the investigation in case it heads in that direction."

Sheriff Turner was thoughtful as he studied me with his weathered face. "What can I do?"

I glanced at Susan, who was also studying me, and said, "Well, I'd like you to deputize Susan and me before we question Pauline. That way, if she tries to fire us we can continue with the investigation and do what we have to do to see it through."

"I see." He shoved his Stetson back in place. "You know if she tries to fire you that would mean she's probably guilty."

"I'm aware."

He thought on it some more, then raised his calloused hand in the air. "Raise your right hands and repeat after me…"

Susan and I each raised our hands and repeated the oath of office for the Chateau Parish Sheriff's Office. Once we were done, Sheriff Turner picked up his cell phone and called his secretary. "Yep," he said when his secretary answered and hollered something at him, "I know I'm supposed to be off, but duty calls. I've just deputized Clint Wolf and Susan Wilson Wolf. I need you to get with personnel and process their commissions immediately." He paused and glanced over his phone. "I assume y'all can pick them up this morning?"

"Yeah," I said. "We have to attend Lance's autopsy and then we'll head right over."

He turned back to his cell phone and told his secretary to have the commission cards and badges ready and waiting by nine o'clock. When he ended the call, he dropped the phone in his shirt pocket. "Now, don't go expecting a check from my office." He laughed, but then stopped abruptly. "Of course, if Pauline does fire y'all, I've got two spots just waiting for the both of you."

"We'll remember that if we find ourselves out of a job." I shook his hand and thanked him. Susan did the same. "Oh, and Sheriff," I said as I reached the door to my cruiser, "thanks for attending our wedding. It meant a lot."

"I wouldn't have missed it for the world."

"So, that's what you had up your sleeve," Susan said when we were jostling up the dirt road, the sheriff's ranch in the rearview mirror. "I've never considered going to work for the sheriff's office before, but I guess it's a real possibility now."

"I hope not," I admitted. "If Pauline's innocent—and God I hope she is—she'll stay out of our way and let us do our job. She knows us well enough to know we'll get down to the truth and figure it out."

"Yeah, well let's hope our luck hasn't run out."

I didn't want to admit that luck sometimes played a role in solving crimes, because, like Susan mentioned, luck had a way of running out—and this was the wrong case for our luck to end.

We didn't say much more on the drive to the coroner's office. We had to wait in the parking lot for fifteen minutes before Doctor Louise Wong arrived. She hurried from her vehicle, struggling to hold her purse, keys, and a large bag while also unlocking the door to the coroner's office.

"It's been a crazy morning," she said as we followed her toward the back of the building. "My kid's throwing up, the babysitter called in sick, and my mom decided to start having chest pains. When I called my husband to tell him to turn around and come back home, I heard his cell phone ringing in the bedroom—and he was halfway to New Orleans." She dropped her things on a desk and opened the door to the morgue. "I swear, I'd win the award for having the worst damn day ever—"

She stopped talking when she saw Lance Beaman's body lying in a supine position on the stainless steel table at the center of the room. "Oh, I stand corrected...Mr. Beaman gets that award."

Doctor Wong's attendant, a young fellow wearing scrubs, shoe covers, a clear plastic face shield, and gloves, quickly moved to her side. "I prepped the body as ordered, Doctor."

She thanked him and garbed out. The first thing she did was a complete and systematic X-raying of the entire body, including very detailed shots of the teeth for positive identification. Once she and her assistant completed the X-ray process, she examined each film carefully and, when done, announced that there were no bullets or other foreign objects inside the body.

As Doctor Wong worked, we told her some of what we knew about the scene and the events leading up to the incident. Throughout it all, I kept my eye on her attendant. He couldn't be older than twenty, but he acted like an old veteran of autopsies. He never flinched and his facial expression remained fixed. I was impressed.

When Doctor Wong was done two hours later, she removed her mask and turned toward Susan and me. "Well, he was definitely alive when the fire happened. Why didn't he try to escape?"

"It looked like the killer threw a Molotov cocktail through each front side window, through the back windshield, and across the front windshield," I explained. "I guess he was boxed in and it got so hot so fast that he wasn't able to do much."

"Extreme heat would make it difficult to do much of anything, and a gasoline and oil fire will certainly produce extreme heat." She tossed her gloves in a biohazard container. "Most fire victims die from carbon monoxide poisoning due to smoke inhalation, but Mr. Beaman died from the flames."

I scowled. "It takes a sick bastard to do that to someone."

"You're correct, and I hope y'all find whoever it is soon, because it's terrifying to think this person is still running around town." Before we left, she told me to find out the name of Lance's dentist so she could obtain his dental records. "Unless you have known samples of his DNA, it's the only way we'll positively identify him."

Once Susan and I were outside in the bright sunlight, I called Justin and told him what we'd learned from the autopsy. He had just left the crime lab in Baton Rouge and was heading back to Mechant Loup.

"I should be there in about four hours," he said. "I need to stop by my house and pack up some clothes. I talked to my supervisor and he authorized me to camp out in town until this investigation is complete. Can you recommend a place to stay?"

"We've got a bed and breakfast in town that serves the best eggs Benedict on either side of the Mississippi. I'll make arrangements with them and get you set up in their best room."

Once I'd ended the call, I asked Susan if she wanted to bring me to the sheriff's office to get our commissions and badges. "I can get my own cruiser," I said, "but if you feel like spending more time with your new husband…"

"I do." She smiled and the dimple that I'd come to love appeared on her left cheek. "I know I'll be married to you for the rest of my life, but the more of that time we spend together, the happier I'll be."

CHAPTER 11

Melvin Saltzman's residence

"Where the hell have you been?" Claire's voice was shrill and it caused Delilah to look up from where she was playing on the living room floor.

"I had to make contact with a potential suspect," Melvin said in a low voice, hoping to help change the tone of the conversation.

"I had to be at work an hour ago, and you knew it!"

"I'm sorry, Honey, but I called and left a message saying I'd be late. I couldn't help it."

"Oh, you could've helped it—you could've easily said you had to come home and watch your daughter so your wife could go to work. You know, it really is that simple, but do you know what the problem is? The problem is you think your job is more important than my job."

"Sweetie, I know your job is important and I respect what you do. It's just that I had to do this. Someone was murdered and I—"

"Oh, right, someone was murdered." Claire folded her arms across her chest and shook her head. "You think I'm just some useless bank teller while you're like a super hero in a uniform. *A murder happened so to hell with Claire's job. She can lose it for all I care.*"

"That's not it at all and you know it." Melvin took a step closer to Claire and frowned. "Look, I had a horrible night and I don't want to fight. I'm really sorry I made you late. If it'll help, I can call your boss and explain that it's my fault, and I'll talk to Susan and let her know that I have to leave work on time from now on."

Without responding, Claire snatched her purse from the table and stormed out the door. Melvin's shoulders slumped and he sank to one of the four chairs around the kitchen table.

"Daddy, is Mommy mad?" Delilah asked, not looking up from the baby doll to which she was trying to force feed a fake plastic chicken leg.

Melvin quickly stood and strode to the living room, where he squatted beside Delilah. "No, Deli, everything's just fine. What're you doing?"

"I'm feeding Princess. She's hungry."

"Okay, why don't you bring her in your room so Daddy can change out of his uniform?"

Delilah looked up and her face scrunched into a ball when she saw the condition of her dad's uniform shirt. "You're dirty, Daddy."

"Yeah, Deli, I had to work hard last night."

"Yeah, you worked hard."

Melvin stood and walked with Delilah to her room, where he secured her child gate in place. When Delilah was first born, Claire had insisted on making three rooms in the house childproof, and she'd made Melvin install child gates and an intercom system so they could always know where she was located in the house and hear what she was doing. For Delilah's third birthday, Melvin tried to convince Claire to let him take down the child gates, saying she was old enough to roam around the house.

"She's been doing hard time for three years," he had said when complaining about what he thought was overkill. "Don't you think it's time she gets out on good behavior? She should at least get trustee status, where she's allowed to walk around the house during the day. I mean, I was playing in the swamps by the time I was one and I drove my first boat when I was her age."

Claire wasn't having any of it, and he was still forced to confine Delilah to her room when he was in the bathroom. He grabbed the intercom and told Delilah to holler if she needed him. She didn't even answer, as she'd plopped down on her bed and went right back to forcing the piece of chicken into the doll's face.

Melvin walked into his bedroom first and removed his pistol from his holster. After unloading it—something he'd never done before Delilah was born—he locked it in his fireproof gun safe. It was a nice safe—could hold a dozen rifles, hundreds of rounds of ammunition, and as many handguns as he could squeeze onto the shelves—and it was one he could never afford. Not long after Delilah had been born, Clint had shown up one day with a dolly and a giant box in the back of his pickup. He'd called Melvin out to the truck to help him and they rolled the beauty into his bedroom.

"Why on earth would you do this?" Melvin had asked.

"Because every cop needs a fireproof safe," was Clint's simple response.

"But what's the occasion? Why would you do this for me?"

"I'm celebrating our friendship," Clint had said, then left as quickly as he had arrived.

After his weapon was secured in the safe, Melvin made his way to the bathroom and placed the intercom on the cabinet. He stared at his face in the mirror. He felt anxious and realized it must be about the argument with Claire. He didn't like arguments, especially if it was between him and his wife. He almost pulled out his phone to call her, but he knew he'd better give her some time to cool off. He certainly didn't want to make things worse.

Melvin pushed the zipper down on his uniform shirt and winced when he caught a whiff of burnt flesh. He quickly stripped it off and rolled it into a ball. He brought it straight to the laundry room, where he tossed it in the washer. He held his breath and stripped off his T-shirt and uniform pants, throwing them in the washer behind the shirt. After putting way too much detergent in the machine, he turned it on, wrapped himself in a towel from the top shelf of the laundry room, and then headed back to the bathroom.

As hard as he tried, he couldn't get the images of Lance Beaman's body burning out of his head, and he kept hearing the agonizing moans of the man as he suffered. Once in the bathroom, he cursed silently when he realized the smell of burning flesh was back. *What if there are soot deposits in my nostrils?*

Thinking quickly, Melvin stepped into the shower. He twisted the water on and turned his head upward, allowing the cool liquid to flow down into his nose. Ignoring every warning he'd heard on the news about the brain-eating amoeba, he snorted the water straight through his nostrils and into his throat, gagging violently as he did so. He bent over, choking and gasping for air. His eyes were blurry from the tears that had formed. After heaving for a few minutes, he was able to catch his breath and he stood to snort more water.

When he was too exhausted to snort more, Melvin took a quick shower and dried off. He pulled on some shorts and a T-shirt and then squirted toothpaste on his toothbrush. As soon as he put the toothbrush to his mouth, he lurched forward and gagged—the toothpaste tasted like burnt flesh. He gagged again, more violently, and then vomited all over the sink.

He fell to his knees, trembling. He was sweating profusely, but he felt cold and afraid. He couldn't catch a deep breath and panic began to set in. "What the hell is wrong with me?" he said out loud. "What's going on?"

CHAPTER 12

Mechant Loup Town Hall

Susan and I stopped outside of Mayor Cain's office and I smiled at her secretary. "Is the mayor in?"

She nodded and buzzed Pauline. "Ma'am, Chief Wilson and Detective Wolf are here to see you."

Before Susan could correct the secretary about her new last name, the door burst open and Pauline waved for us to get inside. She closed the door behind us and we stood there watching as she moved behind her desk. She didn't take her seat. Instead, she started pacing back and forth, her hands folded into a teepee in front of her face. "What's going on with the murder? Do you know anything yet? Who are we thinking did this?"

"Well, as you know, ma'am," I began slowly, "this is a sensitive issue. We, at the police department, have to be careful that we don't appear biased."

She stopped pacing and stared at me. "What are you talking about?"

"I'm sure this won't come as a surprise to you, but there are some who think you might have had a hand in this."

Pauline threw her head back and began laughing. When she glanced back at me and saw my expression, the smile faded rapidly from her face. "Wait—you're not joking?"

"No, I'm afraid not."

"Let me get this straight...someone thinks I want this job bad enough to set a man on fire for it?" She scoffed. "On most days, I want to set *myself* on fire, thanks to having to deal with the childish members of our town council."

"Well, just so we can move forward with the investigation, we have to ask you some formal questions."

Pauline's face was blank. She took her seat and spread her hands across her desk. "Go ahead, then, and ask your formal questions. I've got nothing to hide."

I walked to one of the chairs across from her and sat down. Susan followed my lead.

"Okay, can we start with what you did yesterday?" I asked. "Say, beginning about noon and working your way through the day until this morning?"

"Sure. It was a nice day, so I decided to work in my yard. Since I let Stephen go, I've been doing most of my own landscaping. I weeded the flowerbeds all morning—I know you told me to start at noon, but I'll just give you the rundown of my whole day. Um, so, it was about noon when I took a break for lunch. I drove out to Bad Loup Burgers and got a hamburger, a fry, and a lemonade. I went back home and ate on my back patio—"

The desk phone rang and she answered it, told her secretary to take a message. "Okay, where was I?" She scrunched her lips, then began talking again. "Yeah, I ate lunch on my back patio and then I finished the front flowerbeds. I then took a shower, got dressed, and went to the grocery store. It must've been about four o'clock by then. I bought a bottle of wine, some cheese and crackers, and a ribeye steak. I then came back home, cooked dinner, ate, and went to bed. I didn't wake up until you came knocking on my door this morning."

"How long did you stay at the grocery store?"

"Um, thirty minutes at the most."

"What time was it when you got home?"

"No later than five, five-thirty."

"Did you stop anywhere before going back home?"

"No, I went straight to my house."

I nodded slowly, studying the notes I'd taken while she was talking. "Was anyone with you last night? At your house?"

"No. As you know, I'm a widow and I live alone."

"Yes, ma'am. It'll just help if we can verify as many aspects of your statement as possible."

"And why is that? Am I a suspect?"

I wanted to tell her I didn't think for a second that she was involved, but I couldn't. In order to maintain the integrity of the investigation, I had to treat her just as I would any other suspect. "Well, if I'm looking at this thing objectively, I've got to consider who has the most to gain from Lance's death."

"I already told you that I'd rather set myself on fire than keep this job."

"Yet, you've been running an aggressive campaign trying to defeat him in what's become a very close election. If he were to disappear—or burn to death—it would sure make things easy for you."

"This is true, and I do see your point, but I hope you believe I had nothing to do with his murder." She grabbed her shoulders with opposite hands and shuddered. "The sheer violence of it scares the crap out of me."

"Well, it doesn't matter what I believe." I asked her a few more questions, then turned to Susan. "Anything?"

"Since the incident at the debate, have you and Lance come into contact with each other again?"

Pauline shook her head.

"What was that all about, anyway?"

I wanted to kick myself in the gut for forgetting to ask about the "incident". Susan and I had attended the debate, but neither of us witnessed the exchange in the parking lot. According to two eyewitnesses, Lance was walking to his car when he saw Pauline exit the building. He stepped away from his car and waved Pauline over. When she got close to his car, the witnesses claimed he said something, but they couldn't hear exactly what it was. Pauline cursed him out, but he just laughed, saying, "I bet your husband is turning over in his grave right now."

Pauline had raised her voice and told him to go to hell, to which Lance had responded, "It's all going to come out, Pauline; you just wait and see."

But nothing had come out and no one ever spoke about the incident again. It had happened so long ago that I didn't even think to connect it to the investigation. *Are my subconscious biases already interfering with the investigation? Will I overlook some small detail because I already think I know that Pauline is innocent?* I smiled to myself as I watched Susan questioning Pauline. *Thank God for Susan, because she won't overlook a damn thing.*

"No, we never really spoke again after the debate. I mean, we've run into each other at public events, but we were always cordial to each other."

"What do you think he was talking about?" Susan pressed. "When he said your husband would be turning over in his grave— what do you think he was referring to?"

I saw the lines tighten around Pauline's eyes. "I mean, pick your lie. The man has told so many lies about me that it's hard to keep track of them all. I'm certainly not going to dignify his every lie by trying to defend them."

"Didn't you wonder what he meant when he said it would *all come out*?"

Pauline shrugged. "My life's an open book. When Hays was murdered, the townspeople went through my closet and dragged everything out for the whole world to see. I've got no more secrets— no more skeletons."

Susan was thoughtful, then turned to me and nodded to let me know she was done. I thanked Pauline and we walked outside, where a few clouds had started rolling in from the Gulf.

"Think it'll rain?" I asked once we were back in her vehicle.

"I don't know, but I need some food."

We made a quick stop for lunch at M & P Grill, then headed for Mechant Groceries to corroborate Pauline's account of her activities. The store was located at the corner of a large sugarcane field on the southern end of town and was directly off of Main Street. When we stepped through the sliding doors, I recognized the manager on duty. Her name was Cassandra Billiot and she'd helped me with surveillance footage before with an incident that happened at the store. She greeted us with a smile and a wave.

"How's the lucky couple?" Her face was beaming.

"We're great," Susan said. "We just got back from our honeymoon, but we're already hard at work."

"How'd you know about the wedding?" I asked, dumbfounded.

"Everyone in town knows about the wedding." Cassandra smirked. "You didn't think you could sneak off and have a cruise ship wedding and we not find out about it, did you?"

"I…I guess not," I said.

"Everyone in town is talking about it. All of the men are jealous that you snagged Susan and all of the women are mad that they weren't invited to the wedding."

Hating to be the center of attention, I turned the conversation to the business at hand. "We need to look at some surveillance footage from yesterday. Mainly, the front entrance and the parking lot."

Cassandra looked at Susan. "Is he all business all of the time, or does he let his hair down?"

Susan winked. "He knows how to have fun."

I didn't like the way she said it, because it got Cassandra looking at me all funny and weird.

"The tapes, please?"

"Alright, party pooper, follow me."

Susan and I followed Cassandra through a section of hinged countertop, up a flight of stairs, and into a square office that overlooked the store aisles below. Cassandra sat at her desk and she sucked in air through her teeth while she started accessing the surveillance footage. It made a whistling noise that was annoying. I wanted to say something, but resisted the urge.

She stopped whistling to ask what time we needed her to look up.

"Between four and five in the afternoon."

Cassandra went back to whistling through her teeth while she maneuvered the mouse around and pulled up footage that showed the front entrance. She then split the screen and added a camera that depicted the front parking lot. She started at three-fifty-five and hit the *play* button first, then set it to double speed.

As we watched, people went in and out, all of them empty-handed on the way in and carrying various amounts of groceries on the way out. When the time stamp read four-oh-eight, I saw Pauline sauntering into the store, her phone in one hand and her purse slung across the opposite shoulder. I didn't say anything because I didn't want Cassandra to know we were looking at Pauline, but she took notice.

"Hey, it's Mayor Cain." She suddenly sucked in a mouthful of air. "Oh, wait! Is this about Lance Beaman's murder? One of our customers came in this morning and said Lance was murdered and they said how Pauline was a shoo-in for mayor now that he was dead."

I waved her off, but I was sure my expression was more than a little revealing. "Just keep it going, please. I didn't see what I'm looking for yet."

Just as Mayor Cain had stated, she was only in there for about thirty minutes. She left at four-forty-two carrying two bags, and I could see what looked like the top of a bottle of wine sticking out of one of the bags. I shot a subtle glance at Susan and gave a short nod. Since we were able to corroborate that part of her story, I was comfortable she was being honest about the rest of it. I figured we could ask Cassandra to pull the logs from the register so we could verify the items purchased, but I was certain we had enough. I didn't want to be the cause of more gossip being spread around town.

In order to make Cassandra believe we were looking for something else, I didn't say a word and just let her continue to play the tapes. As the footage rolled, I glanced at the screen on the right and watched as Mayor Cain got into her car. She sat in it for a little over five minutes and I figured she was talking on the phone or texting someone. *Good on her for staying safe,* I thought.

I glanced back at the screen on the left and people were still filing in and out of the store. It was growing a little busier than when the tape first began. I was about to tell Cassandra to pause it when I noticed movement in the screen from the right. It was Mayor Cain driving through the parking lot, headed for Main Street. I stopped and stared when she reached the street. Her right blinker was on. I scowled. She had to turn left to go to her house. As I continued watching, she made a right turn and headed toward the south.

I held my breath, waited for her to turn her car around and head back home. She didn't. Fifteen more minutes of film sped by and I never saw her car again.

Damn! She lied to us!

CHAPTER 13

"Lying doesn't make her a killer," I said about Pauline as Susan was driving us to the hospital in Central Chateau. I stared down at the compact disc in my hands that contained the footage from Mechant Groceries. "And maybe she didn't lie. She could've gone the long way home and still been back by five, five-thirty."

"Clint, that's nonsense and you know it. I understand you feel obligated to give her the benefit of the doubt because of what she did for me, but you've got to stop making excuses for her. She lied to us and we have to find out why." She turned to look at me. "And you're right, just because she lied doesn't mean she killed Lance, but we still need to find out why she lied."

"We don't know for sure that she lied." My mind raced faster than Susan was driving—she was speeding to get to the hospital so we could interview Lance Beaman's wife—as I tried to figure out an explanation for what was in the video. I needed to find another way to determine if Pauline had gone home after leaving the grocery store, some way to verify her story.

We had just crossed the Mechant Loup Bridge when it came to me. "M & P Grill is located at the corner of Kate Drive and Main Street," I said. "They have surveillance cameras outside the restaurant and, if I remember right, some are facing the highway." I nodded for emphasis. "We'll be able to see Pauline leaving her street and then returning."

"And when we prove she didn't return when she says she did?" Susan asked pointedly. "What then?"

I sighed. "Then we sit her back down and find out why."

We rode in silence most of the way to the hospital, each of us lost in our own thoughts. I had stopped worrying about Pauline for the moment and was wondering why Nicole Beaman had requested to speak with us. The office had received a call from someone at the hospital saying that Mrs. Beaman needed to speak with the detectives working her husband's murder, and she needed to see them ASAP. She claimed she had information that was crucial to the case. I wanted to know what that information was and I wanted to know right away.

Thanks to a school bus that had pulled out in front of us while we were traveling through the southern part of Chateau Parish, Susan had been forced to slow down considerably, and then had had to stop every few hundred yards as the bus unloaded. Neither of us liked passing up school buses, so we settled in for the long ride. Finally, the bus turned down a long street and she was able to speed up again. We made it to the hospital a little after three o'clock.

We found Mrs. Beaman in one of the rooms on the second floor and she seemed to be doing well physically, but she was an emotional wreck. I stood back and let Susan take the lead, since she had established something of a rapport with the woman while out at the scene of her husband's murder.

Susan pulled a stool up beside the hospital bed and held Mrs. Beaman's hand and told her how sorry she was about what had happened. The elderly woman cried for a bit, but when she was ready to talk, she cleared her throat and squared her shoulders.

"I know who did this to Lance."

When she paused, Susan nodded and said softly, "Go on…"

"Lance and I tell each other everything, as most married couples do." She paused for a moment to allow her chin to stop trembling, and I'm sure she was realizing that they would never tell each other anything ever again.

"Well, early on in the campaign, he had hired this private investigator to follow Pauline Cain around to try and dig up some dirt on her. He knew she would be hard to beat, so he wanted to find out if she was as clean as she claimed to be. She wasn't and he found out something that could end her career." She took another quivering breath, as though questioning what she was about to do.

I shifted my feet as I stood there waiting, not at all liking where this was going.

When she spoke again, Mrs. Beaman's voice was uncertain. "He made me swear to never utter a word of this, so I feel like I'm betraying his trust."

Yes, I wanted to say, *so shut the hell up and stop spreading lies about a good woman.*

Instead, I just watched while Susan told her to go ahead and tell us everything she knew. "Considering what's happened, I'm sure your husband would want you to share this information with us."

That seemed to give her courage and she continued. "This PI, he's very good at his job. He followed Pauline Cain every day for about a month. He knew all of her patterns. He knew what time she got up in the morning, where she went after she left work, what she liked to eat on Tuesdays—"

"So, basically," I said, interrupting her, "he stalked her."

Susan shot me a hard look and I clamped my mouth shut, mumbled an apology.

"I...I don't feel comfortable telling you any of this in front of him," Mrs. Beaman suddenly said, pointing directly at me. "Lance told me the police department was in the tank for Pauline. He said he spoke to that man and he had taken sides."

Before Susan could say anything, I apologized again and stepped out of the room. Needing some fresh air, I took the elevator down and stepped out onto the sidewalk. I pulled out my phone and called Melvin. When he answered, his voice sounded strange.

"Hey, man, are you okay?" I asked.

"Yeah, I'm just a little tired." He laughed, but I could tell it was forced. "Deli kept me up most of the day, but I'll be fine. I've got until Wednesday to catch up on my sleep."

He had just gotten off of a weekend rotation where he'd worked Friday, Saturday, and Sunday, and he would now be off tonight and tomorrow night. After we talked a little about his daughter, I asked again what he thought about Zack Pitre. "I know you said he was acting strange. Was it strange enough to make you think he was guilty?"

"I don't know," he said thoughtfully. "I don't know if he's smart enough to burn someone alive without setting himself on fire. It seems like he would bungle that kind of job."

"Justin did say it was an amateur job." I scowled. "What about Pauline? Do you think she would have it in her to do this?"

"No way," he said with confidence. "I'll say about Mayor Cain what Zack's mom said about him. She wouldn't hurt a gnat if it landed in her white beans—or something like that."

"Yeah, that's what I'm thinking, too." I was about to end the call but it seemed like there was something on Melvin's mind, because he just sat there breathing, not saying anything and not in a hurry to end the call. "Is everything okay, Melvin?"

"I guess."

"Come on, you can talk to me."

"It's just that Claire got mad at me for getting home late this morning. She said I made her late for work and that I didn't respect her job, that I considered my job more important than hers."

"Oh, damn, Melvin, that's my fault for asking you to go out and make contact with Zack. I'm really sorry. Would it help if I talked to her?"

"Probably not." He sighed. "I guess she'll get over it. I just don't like fighting with her."

"Why don't you go buy her some flowers or something?" I suggested. "It works wonders. Get roses. Red ones. They're like a magic potion that renders most women helpless. As soon as they see those thorny things that'll die inside of a week, they melt and forget why they were mad at you in the first place. Weirdest thing I've ever heard seen."

"Thanks, Clint. I'll do that."

"And have supper cooked when she gets home."

"Got it. Thanks!"

I smiled as I ended the call, but my smile faded when I turned and saw Susan standing there glaring at me. "I know it's not me you're talking about, because you've never bought me red roses, Clint Wolf."

I felt as though I'd parachuted into a mine field and each word I spoke represented a footstep that could get me blown the hell up. "Melvin's having problems with Claire. They're fighting. I was just trying to help him out."

She was quiet for a moment and we each stood there staring down at the ground. I felt horrible, but I didn't know what to say so I simply apologized. She waved me off, but I could still see the hurt in her eyes.

"I know you had a life before me and I know you were married," she explained, "and that was all before I even knew you. I've got no right to complain or be upset, and I can't really explain what I'm feeling or why it bothers me." She shrugged a shoulder. "I guess it just stings a little hearing you talk about your life with another woman."

I groaned inwardly, wanting to kick myself in the groin. I'd barely been married a week and I was already saying things to upset my new bride. "Sue, I'm really sorry. I didn't mean for it to come out that way."

She nodded and walked toward her Tahoe. I followed and

resisted the urge to ask her what Mrs. Beaman had said. I figured when she was ready to talk, she'd tell me all I needed to know.

CHAPTER 14

Susan drove the entire way to our house in silence. I didn't know what to say or do, so I just stared out the window and watched the scenery fly by. When she shut off the engine, I quietly stepped out and rubbed Achilles' head when he rushed to my side. Susan stayed sitting in her vehicle, so I walked inside and retrieved my keys from the hooks near the door.

When I walked back out onto the patio, she was just getting out of the Tahoe. Without saying a word, she walked around the front of the cruiser and directly to me. Wrapping her arms around me, she just buried her face in my chest and held me for a long time. I squeezed her tightly and apologized again.

"No," she said softly, "I'm sorry for getting upset. I'm not the jealous type, so I don't know why it bothered me to hear you talking about buying flowers for your first wife. I guess I just let the information from Mrs. Beaman get the best of me."

I pulled away and stared down at her. "What do you mean? What did she tell you?"

Susan stared directly into my eyes. "She told me Pauline was having an affair."

"She's a widow—she can do whatever the hell she wants."

Her eyes never leaving mine, she said, "According to Lance's investigator, Pauline was having an affair with a married man."

"Who is this investigator?"

"She didn't know his name, only that he was from Mechant Loup and he caught Pauline red-handed sleeping with a married man—someone from town."

I didn't like the way Susan was staring at me, but I didn't dare look away or allow my eyes to waver one bit.

"Who?"

"Lance wouldn't name the person, but he said if Pauline didn't drop out of the race he would expose her." Susan sighed. "Look, I trust you and I'm a confident woman, but I'm not so arrogant to think it could never happen to me. It's happened to better women than me, so I'm not naive. I'm a realist and I understand I can only control one person—and that's me."

"What are you talking about? *What* could never happen to you?"

She lowered her head, stared at the ground. "I don't want to say it out loud."

I put my hand under Susan's chin and gently tilted her head upward. "Don't you ever doubt me, and don't you ever forget that I'm a Wolf...and wolves mate for life."

Her face twisted into a half-frown, half-smile. "I feel embarrassed, but it's just that you've been defending Pauline a lot, even though it's obvious she's up to something. And when I heard you talking about flowers, I started wondering exactly who you'd bought them for, and then there's..."

"What is it?" I asked when her voice trailed off.

"Well, ever since I found out that my dad had cheated on my mom, I've been worried that the same thing could happen to me. To me, he was as perfect a man as there was, and if he could falter, well, I figured anyone could falter."

I didn't know what to say to convince her that I would never cheat on her, so I just held her again. I don't know how long we stood there under our carport, wrapped in each other's arms, but Achilles soon grew tired of us ignoring him. He began barking and running back and forth at our feet.

"What else did Mrs. Beaman say?" I asked when Susan let me go to show Achilles some attention.

"Nothing much, really, other than she thinks Pauline killed Lance to keep him from exposing her."

I remembered the incident that took place after the debate and asked if Mrs. Beaman mentioned what that was about.

"Yeah, she said Lance told Pauline that she'd better drop out of the race or he was going to expose her affair and turn all of the townswomen against her."

In the few years I had been in Mechant Loup, I'd learned that the women in town believed strongly in marriage, family values, and God. When I was chief of police, I'd fielded more than a few complaints from some of these God-fearing women who felt that

Officer Amy Cooke wore her pants way too tight and showed off too much cleavage.

"Can't you make her button up that shirt?" one elderly woman named Mildred had said when she caught me in a diner early one morning. "My Hal's already had two heart attacks and if he sees everything she's got going on up there, well, he might just have number three."

Amy was a good cop and a grown woman, so I wasn't about to tell her how to dress. "Tell Hal to do what I do and he'll be just fine," I'd told Mildred. "He might even live to be ninety."

"And what do you do?" she'd asked heatedly.

"Look her in the eyes."

Mildred had stormed off muttering under her breath. While the women in town were somewhat divided on the issue—most of the town's elders, like Mildred, believed women should dress more conservatively and the younger ladies believed in individual freedom—they were all united when it came to adultery. Given a choice, they would probably enact harsher penalties for adultery than murder, so I knew they would all turn against Pauline if they learned she was sleeping with a married man.

"Do you believe Mrs. Beaman?" I asked Susan.

She shrugged. "I've got no reason to doubt her. She said Lance claimed Pauline threatened him when he said he'd expose her, but she wasn't there to hear it. She thinks Pauline was afraid that Lance would make good on his threat, so she killed him before he could expose her."

I didn't like it one bit, but I knew I'd better not defend Pauline any more. Fact was, the only reason I felt obliged to Pauline was because of what she'd done for the woman I loved. It had nothing to do with Pauline and nothing to do with me...it was all about Susan.

I glanced around the patio. "Well, I guess we'd better get back out there and find out if the surveillance cameras from M & P Grill show Pauline coming and going from her house."

Susan glanced at her phone and shook her head. "That fire marshal should be in town by now, so it's probably better if you got him involved in the case."

"But I need your input," I said. "You're the smartest part of me."

She smiled and rubbed her cool hand against my face. "I love you, Clint."

I moved in and kissed her soft lips. It was a long kiss. When we finally pulled away from each other, her eyes were only half open and she seemed to be purring.

"Does that mean you're coming with me?" I asked.

She opened her eyes and frowned. "No. Three's a crowd. Besides, I've got my own work to do. I'm sure there's a pile of paperwork on my desk just waiting for my attention, and I've got to check on the shelter. The women will probably need more groceries by now."

Susan had asked Takecia to look after the battered women's shelter while we were on our cruise, and Takecia had placed two women and three children in the shelter earlier in the week. The first thing Susan had done when we got home from the cruise was drive to the end of Paradise Place to make contact with the women and let them know they would be safe there. Only after they'd assured her they didn't need anything, she'd returned home and we'd spent the day lounging around until we'd gotten the call about Lance Beaman.

Feeling like a kid whose mom told him he couldn't go play outside, I hung my shoulders and walked toward my unmarked Tahoe. Susan called out to me as I was slipping into the driver's seat. I whipped around, hoping she'd changed her mind.

"I almost forgot to tell you," she said, rushing to her vehicle and jerking a notebook from the back floorboard. She hurried to me, flipping through the pages. "Mrs. Beaman gave me the name of Lance's dentist—it's the office in town. She said he'd recently had a root canal and they took X-rays during that visit."

I waited while Susan found the note and ripped it from her pad. She handed it to me and smiled to let me know everything was okay between us. "I might even have dinner cooked when you get home— you know, make you melt or something like that."

I chuckled and drove out of our driveway, up Paradise Place, and then headed south on Main toward the bed and breakfast where I'd made reservations for Justin. I needed to bring him up to speed on the investigation and we needed to start pulling tape from M & P Grill.

CHAPTER 15

It was almost six o'clock when Justin and I finally left the bed and breakfast and headed up Grace Street in my unmarked Tahoe. Susan had called twenty minutes earlier to say that several news organizations had been calling the office all afternoon, but Lindsey, our daytime dispatcher, had kept them at bay. I knew it wouldn't be long before they were crawling all over the town.

"What time do you shut down for the day?" Justin asked as I slowed to allow a family of obvious tourists—they wore matching shirts that read, *I swam with Godzator: Mechant Loup, LA*—to cross the street.

"I won't shut down until the case is solved and the suspect is in jail," I joked. "Actually, after we get the surveillance footage I was thinking we could head in for the night. I'll make copies on two flash drives. You can view one and I'll view the other and we can compare notes in the morning."

"Sounds good." He rubbed his chin, studying me carefully. "Did you get any sleep since I last saw you earlier this morning?"

I shook my head, wondering what had happened to his neck. When he'd raised his hand, it exposed a thick and nasty burn scar that disappeared around his back and under his collar. I averted my eyes in case he was self-conscious about it.

"I slept enough on my honeymoon to carry me over to next week," I said. "Besides, Susan and I were running down every lead we could as quickly as we could. You know how this goes; the case is like a pot of gumbo, it starts growing cold from the second you take it off the fire. We've got to work fast before this becomes a cold case." I shifted my eyes from the road in front of us to look at him.

"And I don't need to tell you how important it is that we solve this particular case. The man was a candidate for mayor, for Christ's sake. We've been able to dodge the media so far, but that won't last long. I'm betting there will be news vans from all major networks crawling all over town by morning—"

"Not morning...now." Justin pointed to the right. I had stopped at the corner of Grace and Main and looked toward the Mechant Loup Bridge. There, just coming over the crest, was a white news van with a large folding satellite and cameras mounted on top.

I groaned, hoping they wouldn't recognize my vehicle as an unmarked cruiser. The reporter was pointing at something on her phone and the driver was looking where she pointed, so they drove right on by without seeing us. If they were following the online map to the police department, it would take them to the old building about six blocks down the road. We needed to go ten blocks in the same direction and we needed to do it without being seen.

I made sure there were no other vans behind them and then shot straight across the highway, where Grace Street continued west across Main. I drove to the end of Grace, turned south on Jezebel Drive, and then zigzagged through the back streets of town until we reappeared on Main from Lacy Court. M & P Grill was just south of us and on the same side of the street. I looked both ways to make sure the news van wasn't in the area before getting onto the highway.

"It looks clear," Justin said. "I know I'm all turned around and lost as hell. I don't even know which way is up with all the maneuvering you just did."

I shot a thumb over my shoulder as I sped down the highway, pulled into the parking lot, and then drove around to the back of M & P Grill. "That way is north."

"Where do you think the reporters went?"

I told him about the problem with the online map. "They haven't updated it yet, so people from out of town are always driving up to the slab that used to be our building."

"It got burned down, didn't it?" His eyes lit up as though he remembered hearing about it.

I nodded, frowning at the memory of that fateful day.

"I heard Ox talk about it during a presentation at the fire academy. I was there presenting on cause and origin, he was giving one on hazards at a fire scene. He talked about the dangers they had faced because of an active shooter. I think he also mentioned something about live ammunition inside the building."

"Yeah, those firemen risked their lives that day, that's for sure.

We're lucky we didn't lose any of them." I shut off the engine and slipped out of my vehicle, pointed to two cameras in front of the building. "We need the footage from those angles."

Justin stood in the parking lot and surveyed his surroundings, trying to get his bearings. He pointed toward Kate Drive, which was directly adjacent to the south of M & P Grill. "Is that the street Mayor Cain lives on?"

"Yeah." I explained how she would've headed south to go to Mechant Groceries. "I didn't watch the entire footage from the grocery store yet, so I don't know if she drove by the store later, but she definitely didn't pass back in front of the store in time to be home before or during the murder."

Justin rubbed his dark face and shook his head. "That doesn't bode well for her, especially since she lied about being home."

"Well, we don't know for sure if she lied," I corrected. "It's possible she drove the long way around town to get back home, kind of how we did to get here."

He didn't say anything, but he looked skeptical as he followed me into the restaurant. I nodded to the young man who was wiping down a table near the door, introduced myself and Justin. "Is the manager here?"

"Yes, sir. I'll get her." He hurried off, carrying a pile of dishes with him.

It was slow for a Monday night, with only a few tables occupied, and Justin asked if the food was any good.

"As good as it gets. If you plan on eating here, I recommend anything with shrimp in it—I usually get a shrimp on bun—or the fried soft shell crabs on a bed of jasmine rice."

Justin was about to say something when the manager appeared from the door that led to the kitchen. She flashed a bright smile. "Clint, how the hell are you? It's been a minute since I've seen you. I heard you and Susan finally tied the knot."

"We did." After making small talk for a little bit, I introduced her to Justin and explained that we were there to retrieve some surveillance footage.

"Is this about the murder from last night?"

I smiled, turned up my hand. "You know I can't really talk about it."

"No, no, I understand. Follow me."

She led us to the office and showed us to the surveillance system. I reached into my front pocket and produced two flash drives. "Do you mind if I help myself? I know you're busy out there."

"We're not that busy," she said slowly, glancing down at the monitor. She was a nosy one and I didn't want her mentioning what I was after.

"Look, I'll owe you."

She seemed to like the sound of that, and flashed her smile again. "Just let me know when you're done."

When she was gone, I accessed the *Menu* feature on the surveillance system and set out copying everything from the two front cameras between four yesterday afternoon and six this morning. Once I'd copied all of the footage to one flash drive, I then copied it to the other. Next, I shoved each flash drive into a USB port on the computer and checked to make sure the video clips had been copied successfully and were operable.

"Looks like we're good to go," Justin said when the first video began playing.

I nodded and removed the drive from the USB port and handed it to him. "Your homework, if you feel like doing it."

Justin took the flash drive and secured it in his shirt pocket. "I think I'll pick up a six pack and watch these movies all night. Care to join me?"

"Nah, I don't drink anymore." I led the way back into the restaurant and thanked the manager. It had taken about forty minutes to download all of the footage, and the sun was setting when we stepped out into the parking lot. I stopped abruptly when I saw a reporter standing near my vehicle. "Damn it, they found us."

She saw me almost immediately and waved for her cameraman to follow her. "Chief Wolf, is it true that a mayoral candidate has been assassinated?"

I nodded grimly and walked by, ignoring the question. Justin had played this game before, too, and he remained cool as he walked around them and stepped into the passenger seat.

"Chief Wolf," the reporter pressed, "does the murder have anything to do with the election? Is it true that Mayor Pauline Cain is a suspect?"

Where in the hell did they get that? I felt my face tighten, but I tried not to let it show. Once I was in the driver seat and the door was shut, Justin shook his head. "We're not going to be able to keep the lid on this one. If your boss is innocent, she'd better hope we catch the killer before the election, because—right or wrong, guilty or innocent—her political career's about to be in the toilet."

I grunted at the prospect of Zack Pitre becoming the town's next mayor. *What a twist that would be, and damn, would his momma be proud of him.*

I drove to the bed and breakfast and dropped off Justin, then headed home. The news van followed me to the front of Paradise Place and the cameraman rushed out to film me opening my gate. The reporter joined him and began firing off questions. I fixed them with a hard stare. "Don't even think about driving onto my property."

The cameraman gulped and nodded, but the reporter kept shouting her questions. "Are you conflicted, Chief? How can you investigate your own boss? Doesn't she have the power to fire you? And do you think she *will* fire you if she's implicated?"

I drove through the gate, stopped to lock it, then headed to the house, leaving the reporter and cameraman standing with the mosquitoes. I knew it wouldn't take the little winged devils long to find them, so they'd be forced to get back in their van. What they did next was anybody's guess. I said a silent prayer that they didn't know where Pauline lived, because I could easily see them camping outside her house for the night.

Achilles heard my truck before I'd gone a hundred yards. Through the bright headlights, I saw his dark figure racing down the street to meet me. I stopped and leaned over to open the front passenger's door, laughing as he bounded into the vehicle with an excited yelp. He took his place on the seat beside me and sat upright, as proud as he could be. I knew he had to be remembering our days together on the water, back when I was a swamp tour guide. I sighed. I loved police work with every fiber in me, but those days were also fun.

When I pulled into our driveway, I noticed the lights were on in the gym. I walked over and found Susan pounding the heavy bag like it had stolen her lunch. Her bare feet moved gracefully across the canvas and the muscles in her legs rippled with each movement. Although she glided like a dancer, her strikes were violent and the bag seemed to grunt with each contact.

Achilles' bark echoed loudly in the enclosure and Susan whipped around, her eyes narrow and her hands ready. She relaxed and moved away from the bag when she saw us standing there.

"Everything okay?" I was worried she might still be upset from earlier.

"Yeah, I thought I'd try to work off some of the desert I ate on the ship." She snatched a towel from a weight bench and wiped sweat from her face as she approached us. She leaned up and gave me a kiss. Her lips were warm and steam rose from her shoulders and head. "I didn't expect you home so early."

I hefted the flash drive in my hand. "I've got homework—hours of it."

She groaned. "It's not the kind of movie night I was hoping for, but I guess it'll do. Want me to make popcorn?"

"You know I hate popcorn."

She winked. "I'll eat your share."

CHAPTER 16

Melvin Saltzman's house

"Hurry, Deli, take your position...Mommy's home!" Melvin quickly put the last of the silverware on the table and rushed to the living room, where Delilah had curled up on the sofa and pretended to be asleep. Melvin threw himself into the recliner and kicked his feet back just as the front door opened. Although his eyes were closed, he could hear Delilah silently giggling and he knew she was squirming under her blanket. The only other sound he heard was the jingling of keys.

"Okay, if you two are sleeping," Claire asked from the doorway, "then who cooked that wonderful meal I smell?"

Melvin beamed on the inside as he realized Clint had been right. He opened his eyes and stared across the room at his wife. She was staring right back at him, but she wasn't smiling. There was a deep frown on her face. He quickly jumped to his feet. "What is it?"

Claire dabbed at a tear that had slid from her eye and she hurried across the room to greet him. She threw her arms around him and whispered, "I'm so sorry about this morning. I had no idea what you'd been through. Someone at the bank came in and told us."

Melvin swallowed a lump in his throat, tried to hold back the tears. He was relieved that the fight with Claire was over, but he wasn't about to admit that he hadn't slept a wink all day because he couldn't get the image of Lance's horrific murder out of his mind. "It's nothing."

Claire pushed away from him. "*Nothing?* It's horrible! They said you risked your life to save him. That you could've—" Claire broke down crying and buried her face in his chest.

"Mommy, what's the matter?" Delilah asked from the sofa. Melvin glanced over to see the blanket dangling from her head, revealing only one eye and a long pouting face. "Why are you crying?"

"She's just so happy about the food you cooked," Melvin said. "She's crying tears of joy." He tilted Claire's face upward and smiled. "Aren't you, Mommy?"

Claire pushed her lips together in an act of bravery and nodded. She turned to Delilah. "Yes, dear, I'm so happy you cooked for me. I've been working hard and I'm hungry. I'm so happy you cooked." She stepped toward the sofa and tugged the blanket off of Delilah's head. "Now, why don't you show me what's for dinner?"

Delilah jumped from the sofa and grabbed her mother's hand, trying to drag her to the kitchen. "I wanted to make pizza, but Daddy said you like cow bones, so we made you some."

Claire wiped her cheeks and shot a quizzical glance in Melvin's direction.

"T-bones," he explained, "with baked potatoes and salad."

"And roses!" Claire's mouth dropped open and she pulled away from Delilah and examined the vase at the center of the table. "A *dozen* red roses!"

Melvin frowned as he watched her throw her hands to her face and begin crying even more. *Damn, Clint, you didn't tell me this would happen!*

Claire hugged him again, uttering another apology through her sobs. "Now I feel so horrible."

Melvin's eyes misted over, but no one could see. He felt Delilah's little arms wrap around their legs and he dropped a hand to her head. After a few long moments, Claire took a shaky breath and looked around. "I need to go to the bathroom and clean up."

"Take your time," Melvin said. "I'll serve the plates."

Claire disappeared into the short hallway to the bathroom and Melvin snatched a plate off the table. He opened the oven, where he'd placed the steaks to keep them warm after taking them off the grill, and grabbed the tongs from the countertop. He was bending over and reaching for the first steak when the smell of the meat rose up to greet his nostrils. He immediately lurched forward and gagged, as bile rose to his throat.

"What was that?" Claire called from the open bathroom door.

"Daddy got sick," Delilah sang out. "I think he needs some medicine."

"It's okay." Melvin swallowed hard and forced a smile to reassure Delilah he was fine. "I'm not sick."

His hand trembling, Melvin turned his face to take a breath, held it, and then grabbed the steak without looking. He repeated that process two more times and then plopped a baked potato on each plate. It was easier to dish out the salad, but he had to avoid looking at the meat. He'd struggled to grill it, even going so far as to shove vapor rub into his nostrils and working mostly by feel, but he thought the feeling would eventually pass.

What the hell's going on? he wondered. *Have I gone soft?*

He was coating the salads with dressing when Claire appeared from the bathroom. She'd washed off her makeup and changed into her kick-around clothes. She took her seat next to Delilah and began slicing up her meat. "God, it smells so good."

Melvin just stood there staring into space, wondering how he was going to get through dinner. He hadn't eaten anything since the fire, but he wasn't even hungry.

"Honey, are you okay?" There was concern in Claire's voice.

"Um, yeah, I'm just...I don't feel like eating."

"Then why'd you fix yourself a plate?"

He didn't have an answer for her, so he just said he needed to use the restroom. Once inside, he closed and locked the door—something he never did—and stared at his pale face in the mirror. "I don't even recognize you anymore."

He turned on the cold water and splashed a large handful in his face. He tried to sort out his thoughts, going back to the fire and working forward from there. He hadn't felt any fear during the rescue attempt. He had been so intent on getting Lance out of the car that he hadn't even considered what would happen if he got hurt. Afterward, it was a different story. He began imagining Claire's and Delilah's lives without him. He thought about Delilah graduating kindergarten, high school, and college without him being there. What if Claire would've found someone else by then and that someone else would've been there for Delilah? Would she still miss him, or would his memory have faded from her little mind?

That line of thought had segued to his wondering about Lance's children and wife. Who would be there for them now that Lance was dead? And what if Lance was dead because he hadn't tried hard enough to save him? Could he have done more to help the man?

The self-doubt formed in the lower pit of Melvin's stomach and slowly worked its way upward. He felt sick—

"Hey, are you okay in there?" Claire jingled the knob. "What's going on?"

"I just feel sick," he mumbled, sweat forming on his forehead. He felt lightheaded. "I'll be out in a minute."

CHAPTER 17

Four hours later…

Melvin lifted his head from the sofa pillow and glanced over at the clock. It was a little before eleven. After vomiting several times earlier in the night, he'd convinced Claire he had a stomach virus from something he'd eaten. While it didn't stop her from fretting, it did end the relentless interrogation, and Melvin was finally able to stretch out on the sofa to be alone with his thoughts.

At eight-thirty, when Claire had tried to get him to go to bed with her, he'd pretended to be asleep. He'd heard her whisper to Delilah that it was time for bed and the two of them had tiptoed out of the living room. A few minutes later, Claire had returned and softly kissed his head, then tiptoed to bed.

Since that kiss, Melvin had been staring up at the ceiling, listening to the seconds tick by on the wall clock. Still, even after so many hours since the fire, he saw Lance Beaman every time he closed his eyes. A few times during the night he had jerked in his skin when he thought he heard a guttural moan from the front yard. He'd even walked outside the first time and looked around, but nothing was there.

I'm going crazy, he thought. He was smart enough to know that people who went through traumatic events sometimes suffered from post traumatic stress disorder, but he knew that couldn't happen to him. He'd been through a lot in his career as a police officer and nothing had ever bothered him to this extent. *No, it's got to be something else.*

An hour later, and still unable to sleep, Melvin threw his feet to the ground and sat there trying to recreate everything that had happened yesterday morning. He remembered running around trying to save Lance, but he couldn't visualize a blow-by-blow account of his actions. Everything seemed blurry in his mind. He did remember something about a ledger and talking to a man who seemed to be the owner of the house where it happened, but he couldn't remember what the man looked like.

As hard as he tried to remember everything else, Lance's burning body was crystal clear in his mind's eye. *Why is that? Is it because I failed the man?* he wondered. *What if I could've done more to save him?* Melvin suddenly couldn't breathe. *Why didn't I just open the door and pull him out?*

He struggled to remember what the car looked like. As hard as he tried, he couldn't remember why he hadn't simply opened the door and pulled Lance to safety. He strained until his head hurt, but he couldn't remember seeing the door handles. For that matter, he couldn't remember what any of the surrounding area looked like. The only image that stuck was that of the burning body and the awful moaning. *What if there was nothing wrong with the door handles? What if I was too afraid to try to open the door?*

The thought sickened him and he felt like vomiting again. If that was the case, then it *was* his fault that Lance was dead. Feeling dizzy and weak, he sighed heavily and stood to his feet. He needed to see those door handles. If they were intact, he didn't know what he would do with himself. He needed to know the truth and he needed to know now, or he might never sleep again. Maybe if he spent some time out at the scene it would help him work through whatever was going on in his head.

Taking great care not to make any noise, he went to the laundry room and pulled a pair of jeans from a top shelf and slipped them on. He then pulled on his boots and grabbed the keys to his police truck. He hesitated. His pistol was in the gun safe in his bedroom. If he went for it, he might disturb Claire's sleep, but it was a chance he'd have to take. There was a murderer out there and he needed to keep a gun on him at all times.

After quietly retrieving his pistol and the magazine, he stole out of the bedroom and made his way outside, where he loaded his pistol and shoved it in the back of his waistband. He then jumped in his truck and headed to Rupe's Dealership, which was just north of the Mechant Loup Bridge, and it was where Lance's car had been towed. Randall Rupe had been the original owner of the dealership before he died, and it was now being operated by his wife.

Once at the dealership, Melvin parked his truck in front of the building and grabbed a flashlight before walking around to the back, where the storage yard was located. Shoving the flashlight in his back pocket and making sure his pistol was secure in his belt, he scaled the chain link fence and dropped down on the other side. He pulled out the flashlight and made his way through the dark shadows, searching for the burnt car. He found it in a covered area all alone, wrapped in crime scene tape.

His stomach was in knots and his hands were sweating. He was afraid to look, but he knew he had to. Taking one uncertain step at a time, as though the car were a bomb that might go off, he picked his way through the gravel lot. He stopped when he was close enough to see the car. With a trembling hand, he aimed the flashlight forward, but kept his eyes trained on the ground. Finally, he slowly lifted his head, bracing himself for what he would find—

Melvin let out an audible gulp of relief that sounded animalistic and he dropped to his knees when he saw that the door handles were nothing but a melted mess. It took him a few long minutes to recover from the revelation. While there was still a lingering doubt that he could've done more, he felt a little more relieved. He pulled himself slowly to his feet and approached the car. He took his time, examining every inch of the car.

"Damn," he said out loud, "I didn't remember it being this bad."

It was apparent that the fire department had used their "jaws of life" tool to free Lance from the melted mess. Melvin hadn't remembered seeing any of it. Everything had seemed like a bright blur of light emitting from the floodlights and he had wanted to distance himself from the immediate scene.

He took a calming breath and walked away, making a mental note to revisit the place if he ever started having doubts about his actions. He drove toward Mechant Loup-North and flipped off his headlights as he reached the end of North Boulevard, where the burn stains were still prevalent on the street. Not wanting to rouse the occupants of the mansion, he stepped out of his truck and eased the door shut, careful not to make a sound.

Moving by the distant glow from the mansion lights, he studied the ground where Lance's car had been, then the truck that his car had crashed into—it didn't look like it had been moved—and then he moved toward the curb. Taking out his flashlight and aiming the beam of light skyward, he studied the tree branches above.

"Damn, the fire was hot." He hadn't remembered the trees being on fire, but many of the branches were charred. Feeling a little better about his efforts, he sighed deeply and started to return to his truck—

A branch suddenly snapped behind him. He whirled around, stabbing the darkness with his light and reaching for his pistol. "Who's there?"

A brilliant orange glow suddenly flashed from the shadows of the trees and the violent explosion of a gunshot startled him. Not even knowing if he was hit, Melvin dropped to the ground and scrambled frantically toward his truck. Before he could reach it, another shot was fired. Specks of pulverized concrete peppered the right side of his face. Melvin remembered reaching for his pistol when he had heard the branch snap, but he didn't realize it was in his hand until that moment.

Knowing he would never make it to his truck in time and that the next bullet would probably end him, he rotated around until his feet were facing the clumps of trees from whence the shots were being fired.

Lying on his back and aiming between his feet, he fired three shots in quick succession, trying to spray the area from which the gunshots had come. He then pushed off with his right foot and rolled twice toward his truck. He stopped and fired three more shots in the direction of the shooter, then rolled toward his truck again. After shooting and performing one last roll, he finally reached the truck and scurried around to the front bumper, putting the engine block between him and the shooter.

"Who the hell are you?" he hollered, surprised by how calm his voice sounded. He was trembling on the inside. With his back against the truck, he scanned the area to his right and left. What if the shooter was circling around in the darkness, trying to get a bead on him? "I've got backup coming! They'll be here any minute and they're going to kill you! The only chance you've got to make it out of here alive is to throw down your gun and come out where I can see you!"

The shooter didn't reply and Melvin was unable to detect movement from anywhere. It could mean the shooter was gone, or it could mean the person was skilled at stealth movement.

Melvin did a quick mental inventory and realized he'd fired nine rounds from his fifteen-round magazine, which left him with six bullets. He cursed himself silently for not topping off his mag after cycling a round into the chamber earlier at home, but he hadn't wanted to return to the bedroom and risk waking Claire.

When he hadn't heard anything in several minutes, he turned to peek around the front driver side corner of his truck. A gunshot immediately exploded from the trees and he heard the subtle *thunk* of lead penetrating soft metal. He quickly retracted his head and muttered some profanity, first directed at the shooter, and then at himself for not considering earlier that the killer might return to the scene.

Melvin licked his lips, trying to come up with a plan. There was a deep drainage ditch to the south that paralleled the boulevard. If he made a run for it and reached the ditch, he would be home free, but the chances of him getting mowed down were too great. *Damn, boy,* he thought, *this might be it for you.*

A thought occurred to him. If he died out here, Claire would forever wonder why he'd left the house without telling her. She would wonder what he was doing out here, as would everyone, and she would wonder about his behavior earlier in the day. He suddenly gritted his teeth. There was no way he could go out like this and leave her with questions.

After taking a deep breath, he quickly rolled to his feet and maintained a deep squat, careful not to raise his head above the hood of his truck. One small side-step at a time, he scooted toward the passenger side of his truck. His phone was on the center console and his shotgun was secured in the mount near the inside of the passenger seat. If he could get to them, this would all be over in minutes. He'd call for backup and then start blasting that son of a—

He suddenly cocked his head to the side, listening intently. A soft breeze blew in from the south, carrying with it the sound of sirens. He smiled. Someone had heard the shots and called the police department. "They're coming for you!" he shouted. "Your ass is mine!"

Suddenly, gunshots erupted from the trees in rapid succession and bullets began smacking into his truck. It seemed as though the bullets were impacting the driver side, so he scurried closer to the passenger side and hunkered down, praying he wouldn't be hit by a random round. As he squatted there—his pistol gripped tightly in both hands—he had a daunting revelation: the shooter was rushing his position!

CHAPTER 18

Tuesday, April 25
Clint and Susan's house

It was a little after one in the morning and I was still sitting up in bed with my laptop, poring over the surveillance footage from M & P Grill. Susan and I had showered earlier and then retired to the bedroom together, me to get some work done and her to finish reading *Night Over The Solomons* by Louis L'Amour. She'd begun the book while we were on the cruise, but hadn't had a chance to finish it—and she wasn't going to finish it tonight. I don't think she'd flipped two pages before I heard her breathing drop to a low and steady whisper.

I was tired, too, and wanted to call it a night, but I needed to know what time Pauline returned to her house after leaving the grocery store on Sunday evening. I'd already viewed enough tape to know she wasn't home at the time of the murder, so her alibi was mud. I was just finishing up the three o'clock hour on the tape when Susan's phone began ringing from the other side of the bed. I had never answered her phone before, but I was tempted to do so now. I wanted to tell whoever it was to leave her the hell alone and let her get some sleep. I was too late.

"What's going on?" Susan pushed to one elbow. Thanks to the glow from my laptop, I could see her staring through squinting eyes. She looked disoriented. "Why's the alarm going off? It's not six o'clock yet."

I tried not to laugh. "It's your phone, honey."

Groaning, she rolled to the opposite edge of the bed and fumbled around in the dark, trying to locate her phone on the end table. I heard something hit the floor and then I heard her curse. She lunged forward, nearly sliding off the bed, and then gave a triumphant cry when she came up with it in her hand, holding it like a war chief who'd just taken a prized scalp. She cursed again when it stopped ringing before she could answer it. "Oh, it's the office," she muttered. "What the hell do they want?"

She rubbed her eyes to see better and then fumbled with the screen, trying to call them back. Before she could initiate the call, the phone started ringing again. "Hey, this is Susan, what's up?" I saw her sit straight up in bed, fully alert. "Well, who's doing the shooting?" She paused to listen to the nightshift dispatcher, who was Marsha. "Is anyone down?" She paused to listen. "Okay, we're heading that way pronto."

I was out of the bed and already sliding into my jeans by the time she hung up the phone.

"There's some kind of gun battle going down in Mechant Loup-North," she said, pulling on her bra and then searching her closet for some jeans. "Chet Robichaux called and said he heard two gunshots from one gun, and then he heard about ten shots from what sounded like another gun." After her jeans were buttoned, she grabbed her boots, turned them upside down to shake them out, and then shoved her feet inside. "He thinks it's a genuine shootout."

I chased Susan down the stairway. "Is anyone down?"

"He doesn't know. He was going to retrieve his shotgun and go outside, but Marsha told him to stay inside and wait for Amy."

"Is your unit okay?" she asked when we rushed out the door. "I need gas."

I nodded and we both climbed into my unmarked. "Does Amy have backup?"

"Marsha called the sheriff's office and they're sending a deputy, but we'll probably get there first."

She was right, because I was already turning off of Paradise Place and heading north on Main, driving as fast as my Tahoe could go. There was no traffic along Main Street at this hour, and I was happy for that. It allowed me to push the engine to its limit. I was also happy that the news van was nowhere to be seen. Maybe they had gotten tired of getting the runaround and decided to leave town.

I was approaching the Mechant Loup Bridge when the radio scratched to life and Amy's excited voice came through. Her siren was blaring in the background, but we heard her plainly: "Headquarters, I'm ninety-seven [on the scene] on North Boulevard and heading to the back. I hear gunshots! I repeat…shots fired!"

I touched the brakes when we hit the ramp to the bridge, but it didn't slow us down enough to cushion the blow. The jolt was so rough my head would've hit the ceiling had I not been strapped in. Susan threw both hands to the dash and held on for dear life. I muttered an apology and started slowing as we approached North Boulevard. My tires screeched as I made the turn.

"There!" Susan pointed toward the end of the street, where we could see the blue lights flashing on Amy's cruiser. As we sped forward, we could see a truck parked in the middle of the right side of the boulevard. "Oh, my God, that's Melvin's truck!"

I smashed the brakes and my vehicle screeched to a stop. Susan and I bailed and took a quick glance around. There was no one in sight. I hurried to Melvin's truck, but lurched to a stop when I saw that the entire driver side was peppered with bullet holes. The ground was littered with spent shell casings. "Susan, you've got to see this!"

She joined me and her mouth dropped open. My heart racing in my chest, I moved closer and glanced through the driver window. Relief flooded over me. "It's empty."

"Amy!" Susan called, walking toward the cluster of trees, her pistol in hand. "Melvin!"

I fanned out to her right and crossed the boulevard, shining my light across the property surrounding the mansion, but I didn't see any signs of Amy or Melvin. Susan tried calling Amy on the radio, but there was no response.

As Susan made her way through the cluster of trees, I walked around it and searched the outer edges, keeping my pistol at the ready. There was nothing to indicate anyone had been there. I shined my light on the ground, but the dew in that area had not been disturbed. I could hear some rustling in the trees to my left and I called out softly.

"It's me," Susan replied. "There're some snapped twigs and crunched leaves and I found two spent shell casings, but there's no sign of anyone."

I had reached the edge of the mansion property and still hadn't seen any signs of life. I was about to turn and go back when Susan broke through the trees and crossed the street to stand with me.

"They've got to be out here somewhere," she said.

I began walking a little farther toward the front of the street, scanning the property on the north side of the boulevard with my flashlight, when Susan grabbed my arm and pointed. "There…in the grass!"

I looked where she pointed and could clearly see oblong marks in the wet grass that represented footsteps. There appeared to be three distinct sets of tracks and they all led north through an empty field that separated the mansion from the next house on the boulevard. Before we could take another step, we heard a gunshot off in the distance, and it propelled both of us forward.

We raced across the open field, the beam from our flashlights jostling up and down, following the blotches in the dew as best we could. As we ran, Susan repeatedly keyed up her radio and called out to Amy, asking for a status and for her location. We didn't hear any more gunshots and that scared me more than anything.

The footsteps in the dew cut a wide path around the mansion and then headed east, traveling parallel to a barbed wire fence. I heard cows mooing, but couldn't see much of anything. The beams from our flashlights seemed like faded streaks of yellow fingers against the utter darkness that surrounded us. The grass was taller now and I felt it whipping against my pant legs as we ran. It was also easier to follow the trail now, thanks to the deep impression in the grassy field.

Susan was a little ahead of me and I could hear her footsteps pounding the ground and could see her flashlight swing up and down. All of a sudden, her light went airborne and I heard her screech. Before I could react, I slammed right into her back, my chin making direct contact with the back of her head. We both crumbled forward, rolling over and over, tangled up in each other's limbs. When we finally came to rest, I was face down in the wet grass and Susan's left boot was almost in my mouth.

"Are you okay?" I asked, twisting around to try and untie myself from her. My chin hurt something awful, but I didn't have time to worry about that. "What happened? Why'd you stop?"

Susan rolled gracefully to her belly and jumped to her feet. "I saw water up ahead."

I followed her forward and, thanks to the faint glow from the moon, I was able to see that the tall grass ended abruptly at the muddy banks of a drainage canal. "Where's your light?" I whispered. Mine had flown from my hand when we crashed, but my pistol was still clutched firmly in my strong hand. I aimed it toward the banks of the canal.

Before Susan could answer, we were blinded by bright lights, and an authoritative voice shouted, "Put your hands where we can see them!"

CHAPTER 19

"Oh, damn, it's Susan and Clint!" The second voice was Melvin's, and the first had been Amy's. The lights dipped quickly and Amy hollered an apology from across the drainage canal.

I shaded my eyes and saw them standing in the thick grass on the opposite bank. They were both drenched and looked like wet muskrats, their clothes and hair plastered to their bodies.

"What's going on?" I asked Melvin, shining my light up and down the opposite bank, expecting to either see someone in handcuffs or bleeding out. I saw neither. "Who shot up your truck?"

"I don't know. I never saw him." Melvin glanced over at Amy. "But she did."

Amy nodded, brushed a strand of wet blonde hair away from her right eye. "When I arrived at the end of the street, I saw a masked man running toward Melvin's truck, firing as he ran. I gunned my engine and headed straight for him, planning to run him down. Before I got him, he turned and sprinted across the road, jumped the ditch."

"Where is he now?" I wanted to know.

Amy shot her flashlight down the canal, pinpointing the light on a weeping willow tree about fifty yards south of us and on their side of the canal. "Last we saw, he crawled out of the canal near that tree and disappeared in the swamps."

Susan shot a glance in my direction and I nodded. She got on her radio and asked Marsha to call the sheriff's office and request that they put their helicopter in the air. "And request K-9 support and a boat," she told Marsha before clipping the radio back to her belt.

"I fired a shot at him from the water," Melvin offered, "but I doubt I hit him."

Susan shined her light up and down Amy's uniform. It was plastered to her body like shrink wrap, and water was still dripping from the dead radio clipped to her belt. "Y'all tried to swim after him?"

Although the light was dim, I could see redness move over Amy's face live a wave of sunshine. "No, um, we…we didn't see the water in time and ran straight into it. I didn't know what the hell had happened."

"Yeah, she almost drowned." Melvin chuckled a little, but stopped when Amy shot him a cold stare.

"I already told you, I didn't almost drown. I sucked in some water, but I was fine."

Melvin nodded and created some distance between them before saying, "You tell it your way and I'll tell it the way it happened."

Although Melvin was acting like his usual jovial self, there was a look of sadness in his eyes that couldn't be denied. I wanted to ask him what he had been doing out here at this time of night, but resisted the urge. I certainly didn't want to have that conversation with him across twenty feet of muddy water.

Susan moved close to me, turned her back to the canal, and whispered so only I could hear. "Melvin wasn't working tonight. What the hell was he doing out here?"

"Your guess is as good as mine," I whispered back.

She glanced over her shoulder to where Amy and Melvin were squatting near a tree. Their attention was on the swamps to the south, and they were far enough away that they didn't even know we were talking. "Mrs. Beaman said Pauline was having an affair with a married man. You don't think that married man—"

"Sue, don't even say it."

"Melvin's as loyal as they come, Clint, and you know it. He adores Pauline. If he was having an affair with her and she asked him to take out the competition—"

"Damn it, Sue, don't go there." I wiped my face and looked away, not wanting to consider what she was saying.

"Someone has to," she said softly, "because you don't seem to want to go anywhere that makes you feel uncomfortable."

I was quiet for a long moment as sirens wailed in the distance and drew closer. Before long, blue and red lights could be seen in the area of the mansion. Susan picked up her radio and switched to the sheriff's office channel, telling the deputies where to find us.

"It's not that I don't want to go there," I explained when she was done with her directions. "It's just that I know Melvin well enough to know he'd never cheat on Claire."

"Well, I hope you're right."

I sighed. "Me, too."

CHAPTER 20

Within thirty minutes the entire area was flooding with K-9 officers, water patrol deputies, and SWAT members. We had the place wrapped up so tight that a single mosquito couldn't escape. I just hoped the shooter hadn't already made it outside of the perimeter we'd established.

With Susan leading the search effort for the suspect, I had called Justin to meet me at the scene. We were now standing with Melvin on the outside of the yellow crime scene tape near his truck.

"Go ahead and tell Justin what you told me earlier," I said to Melvin, "so he can catch up."

Melvin hesitated.

"It's okay," I said. "He's been there, too, I'm sure."

Justin nodded. "No matter what it is, I'm sure I can relate. I might be a fire investigator, but I worked for the sheriff's office back in the day and I'm still a cop."

Melvin took a deep breath and exhaled slowly. "Okay, so I couldn't sleep because I kept seeing Lance Beaman burning up. Every time I closed my eyes I'd see his face, and I even saw it sometimes when my eyes were open. I started to question my actions at the scene, doubting that I'd done enough to save him." He paused, wiped his face with a hand that shook. "I know it sounds crazy."

"Not at all...I've been there." Justin's voice was soothing. "When I was a young firefighter, a kid died in a house fire in Central Chateau because I couldn't find him. I heard him screaming, so I went searching for him. I went the wrong way down the hall and he died, but I made it out of there alive. I questioned whether or not I went the wrong way on purpose, just to save myself."

"Did you ever get over it?"

"Well, I got some help with it and it got easier to deal with over time, but that kind of thing stays with you. With some things, it's a daily struggle."

Melvin frowned and hung his head. After being thoughtful for a while, he continued telling how he'd visited the storage yard at Rupe's Dealership and then came here to revisit the scene in hopes of getting some closure. When he detailed the shooting that ensued, Justin scowled. "You mean he attacked your position?"

"Yeah. If Amy hadn't shown up, well, I don't know how things would've ended."

Justin looked at me, then back at Melvin. When Melvin had finished his story and walked off, Justin hissed, "This person was trying to kill your officer!"

I nodded my agreement.

"Do you think it's the arsonist?" Justin asked. "And if so, why on earth would he try to kill Officer Saltzman?"

I pointed to the clump of trees. "Melvin first heard the shooter in those trees. I'm betting they lost something in those trees when they attacked Lance. I don't know if they found it or not, but it was important enough to kill a cop over, so we're not leaving until we know for sure what it is."

"But we already searched that area."

"We did, but what were we searching for?"

Justin stared blankly at me. "I don't know—anything that might be evidence in the case."

"Right, we were looking for anything that *might* be there, but now we're looking for something that we *know* is there. I've got metal detectors in the back of my Tahoe. We're going to run them through those trees and we're not going to stop until we dig up every little thing that makes them beep." I pointed to Melvin's truck. "But first, we have to process this shooting scene."

Justin followed me to my vehicle and I removed my crime scene box from the back and we started measuring the scene. We had been working for about twenty minutes when I heard the rhythmic chopping of helicopter blades approaching. I stopped what I was doing and watched the large eyeball of light approaching in the dark skies from the north.

Justin straightened from the casing we were measuring and stood there watching me. "You want to be out there searching for this prick, don't you?"

"Yeah, I do, but I'm in charge of investigations around here, so…" I allowed my voice to trail off and went on to the next shell casing.

It was easy to distinguish between Melvin's shots and those of the killer, because Melvin was shooting a .40 caliber pistol while the killer used a 9 mm. We located nine .40 caliber spent casings and fourteen 9 mm casings.

"You know what I don't understand," Justin said when we moved on to documenting the eleven bullet holes in Melvin's truck. "Why would an arsonist use a gun to try and kill Officer Saltzman? Why not set him on fire like he did with Lance?"

I mulled over what he said for a few seconds. When I opened my mouth to answer, I clamped it shut as a light bulb went off in my head. "I think I've got it!"

"What is it?"

"Your question is backwards."

A blank expression fell upon his face. "Should Officer Saltzman have tried to burn the shooter?"

"No…if the killer has a pistol, then why in the hell would he firebomb Lance? Why not just shoot him like a normal person would?"

Realization caused Justin's mouth to slowly drop open. "Either we're dealing with two suspects—a shooter and an arsonist—or someone was so pissed off at Lance that they wanted to torture him."

I shot my index finger in Justin's direction. "That's exactly what I'm thinking!"

"But what would piss someone off so bad that they'd set fire to another human being? It's such a horrible way to go."

I shot my index finger in Justin's direction again. "*That* I don't know."

He grinned and helped me collect the casings from the scene. Once they were all packaged separately and secured in the back of my unmarked unit, I pulled out my phone and called Susan. The sun was just starting to rise and our surroundings were slowly coming into view.

"Anything?" I asked when she answered.

"Not so far. The dog picked up the scent near the tree Amy and Melvin pointed out and followed the trail for about a mile along the bank, but then it turned back toward the water. It appears the shooter jumped back into the canal—we even found deep boot prints in the mud—but we can't find where he or *she* climbed out."

The way Susan said *she* led me to believe she still suspected Pauline. I told her our theory about a possible revenge motive.

"It makes sense," she said. "Lance said a lot of horrible things about Pauline, and if he was about to reveal her affair, well, she would want revenge." After a slight pause to tell someone to check inside a rotted-out log, Susan asked about the surveillance footage. "Did you ever find out what time she got back home?"

"No." I noticed Justin leaning in the back of my vehicle to get one of the metal detectors. "I've got to go. Be safe."

"We need to find out who Pauline was sleeping with," she called out as I was hanging up. Although she couldn't see me, I nodded.

When I walked over to Justin, he was flipping switches and studying the tiny control panel. "How the hell does this thing work?"

I leaned forward and showed him how to turn it on. He thanked me and waved the search coil near my bumper. It beeped loudly when he drew to within a few inches of the metal. "It works."

I grabbed the other detector, slammed the gate, locked it, and followed Justin to the clump of trees. "So, did you have a chance to finish viewing the surveillance footage?" I asked when we reached the edge of the curb. "I made it to the three o'clock hour when we got the call about this shooting."

"I did finish the tapes." He adjusted his forearm on the stabilizer, nodded to himself when he found the sweet spot. "Yeah, Mayor Cain's vehicle turned down her street at about four-thirty in the morning. She was traveling from the north, so she must've gone through town as you suggested earlier."

I pointed to the right to indicate I'd work that side and pondered this new information as I allowed the search coil to hover a few inches from the ground. "She must've been seeing her boyfriend."

"Yeah, we need to find out who he is." Justin's metal detector beeped and he dropped to his knees to investigate the alert. After a moment of digging through the pine needles and dirt, he pulled up a foil gum wrapper and scowled. He shoved it in his pocket and continued searching. "Any idea who it could be?"

Evil thoughts kept running through my mind, such as the possibility that Melvin had staged the shooting of his own truck to throw the scent off of him and Pauline, but I immediately dismissed it. There was no way Melvin was cheating on Claire. I just knew it. "No, I've got no idea who it could be, but I do know where we can start."

Justin looked up from another miniature excavation he was working on. "And where's that?"

"Mrs. Beaman said a private investigator was following Pauline. While she didn't know his name, she said he was from Mechant

Loup, and we've only got one private investigator in town—" My metal detector finally beeped and I dropped to my knees to investigate the alert. After removing a thick blanket of dried leaves, I found a rusted bottle cap. *Damn it!*

We continued searching and had moved about twenty feet from the curb. It was a painstaking process, because there were tons of tiny pieces of metal in the dirt. In addition to bottle caps and gum wrappers, there were nails, pieces of rebar, and even an old zipper.

The sun was clawing its way up the eastern horizon and we were both dripping sweat. It was only April, but the temperature was already into the eighties and the humidity was in the nineties. Forecasters were predicting a hot summer—probably the hottest on record—but I didn't care. Anything was better than the cold weather.

I had moved around a large pine tree and was just waving the search coil of the detector between the edge of a crawfish hole and the tree when it beeped. Expecting another piece of trash metal, I leaned forward and brushed the leaves away. There was nothing. I swept the metal detector over the area again, and once again it beeped. I was about to lean forward to start digging in the ground when something shiny in the crawfish hole caught my eye.

"Holy smokes!"

CHAPTER 21

Justin dropped his metal detector and rushed to my side. "What is it?"

I pointed to the center of the muddy mound in the ground. "Look down in the crawfish hole."

Justin craned his neck to see and then gasped. "A cigarette lighter!"

"Yep, the arsonist must've lost his lighter during the attack on Lance and then came back for it."

"And Officer Saltzman interrupted him—or her."

I nodded, straightened to retrieve my camera and measuring tape. Once I'd photographed it and then measured the location, I pulled on some latex gloves and carefully removed the brass lighter—it looked like a Zippo—from the crawfish hole. It was faded and there was mud smeared on the side, but I didn't attempt to clean it. This was a job for the crime lab. I needed them to process it for prints and DNA, because this might be the best chance we'd have of identifying the killer. I doubted they would be able to recover DNA or prints from the small pieces of glass we'd recovered, so this lighter was now our best piece of evidence.

"Do you want me to bring it to the lab?" Justin asked. "I can be back by noon if I leave now, and I can get them to put a rush on processing it."

I didn't even stop to consider the offer. There was still so much to do around here and I didn't have time to take a trip to Baton Rouge. I signed the chain of custody label on the evidence package and handed it right to him. "I'll keep you posted on what happens with the search."

He nodded and hurried away, cradling the evidence package like it was gold. If it contained the evidence that would lead us to the killer, it was better than gold.

I picked up my gear while the tow truck hooked up Melvin's cruiser. "Where to?" the driver asked.

"The police department. You can follow me, but wait just a second." I walked over to where I'd seen Melvin sitting on the tailgate of a sheriff's office water patrol truck. "Ready to go?"

He looked up from his phone. "Yeah, as ready as ever, I guess."

Once we were in my Tahoe and the wrecker truck was following us out of the neighborhood, I asked if he needed anything.

"Nah, I'm fine." He stared out the window, never making eye contact with me. "I just need some rest."

I remembered how I'd dealt with my inability to sleep when I'd lost my wife and daughter and what it had done to me, so I cautioned him against turning to alcohol.

"I'm not that upset about it," he said. "This is nothing compared to losing your wife and child. It's just that I doubted myself for a bit and I wondered if I'd done everything I could, but I feel better knowing that the doorknobs were melted off."

"Well, if you need someone to talk to, don't hesitate to call me— and I don't care what time of the day or night it is. You ring my phone, and I'll be there."

He forced a grin. "I appreciate that. I really do."

Once we'd led the wrecker to the police department and had secured Melvin's truck under the building—the place was constructed of solid concrete to withstand hurricanes and it had been raised twelve feet off the ground to avoid possible floods—I took Melvin home.

Claire was sitting outside on the steps when I pulled into their driveway. She rushed to my Tahoe and nearly tackled Melvin at the door. She was crying and the words that gushed from her mouth were jumbled and incoherent, but I caught an apology somewhere in the midst of the chaos.

"It's okay," Melvin said. "Everything's fine now."

"But you could've been killed!"

"I could be killed on any given day, Claire. It's the nature of the job."

She pushed off of him and crossed her arms in front of her chest. "And that's supposed to make me feel better?"

"No, but this will…" He scooped her up in his thick arms and dipped her low, planting a kiss on her lips.

She giggled through the tears and fussed him for doing that in front of me. I just sat there in silence, watching the two of them interact. I knew there was no way in hell he'd ever cheat on her—not with Pauline, and not with anyone else. I frowned, stared at my hands on the steering wheel. Pauline had apparently cheated with someone and she had definitely lied to me, so she had some explaining to do. First, though, I had to pick up Lance's dental records and get them over to Doctor Wong for the sake of completeness, and I had to check on Susan.

When Melvin finally turned and grabbed his gear from the back seat, I waved to him and Claire and drove away. Traffic was heavy, so it took longer than I liked to make it the few blocks to the dentist's office. When I told them what I needed, they informed me they would contact Doctor Wong and send the records to her electronically—something about privacy laws—so I thanked them and left. Before driving away, I called Susan.

"We still haven't found anything," she said, sounding frustrated. "He either slipped away or drowned. Either way, I'm about to call off the search. I think we're just wasting time at this point."

"Okay, I'm heading to meet with Francis Allard. He's the only private investigator in town, so it's got to be him."

There was a long pause. I thought we got disconnected.

"Susan, are you there?"

"Yeah, I'm here."

"Oh, I thought I lost you. I said I'm going meet with Francis Allard."

"I heard you." She sighed. "Who do you think Pauline was sleeping with?"

"I've got no clue, but I have a feeling I'm about to find out."

"Let me know, will you?"

"Sure thing."

CHAPTER 22

Francis Allard lived off of Coconut Lane. I found his small white house with the manicured lawn on the left side of the street. There was a camper parked on the side of the street in front of his house, and I wondered how often he used it. I'd heard of him and knew he was an ex-homicide detective from New Orleans who had retired after twenty-five years of service. He'd moved to Mechant Loup ten years ago and opened a private investigations business to supplement his pension. I'd never met him, but that was about to change.

I walked up the narrow sidewalk and knocked on the door, studying his yard as I waited. From the looks of it, Francis spent his time cutting the blades of each grass with a scissor. I was far from retirement, so I had no clue what I'd do once I got there, but it appeared that keeping a manicured yard was a requirement.

"Clint Wolf," said Francis when he opened the door. He extended his hand. He was a short man, barely rising to five-foot-five in his shoes, and his gray hair and moustache betrayed his age, which had to be barreling down on sixty. Despite his age, he was wiry and he appeared to still have some fight in him. "What the hell can I do for you?"

His accent was thick and sounded like most cops I knew from New Orleans. "Can I come inside and talk?" I asked.

Shifting the collar on his button-down fishing shirt, Francis glanced over his shoulder. "My wife works nights. She just got to bed, so we'll talk in my office."

He pulled the door shut and walked around the eastern end of his house and I followed him down a long driveway that extended toward the back yard. At the end of the drive, there was a shed-looking building that had an air conditioning unit in the window and a padlock on the door. A small faded sign that read "F. Allard, PI" hung over the door.

I didn't expect much when Francis pushed open the door, so I wasn't disappointed to find a small desk, a chair on either side of it, and two large filing cabinets against the wall to the left.

"Please," he indicated with his hand toward the chair in front of me and scooted around the desk, "have a seat."

The air in the confined space was stale and smothering. As we sat across from each other, he leaned back and turned on the a/c, then apologized for the heat. "Had I known I'd be having company, I would've turned it on earlier to cool off the place. So, what's this all about?"

I shot a thumb toward the front of his house. "How often do you take the camper out?"

"Is that what this is about?" He chuckled. "You want to make me an offer on that old thing? I tell you this; I'd be committing a theft if I took five grand from you. That damn thing hasn't moved in two years. We keep it clean for when we get the money to get it running again, but so far it doesn't look like that'll happen this year, or the next. I don't know if you realize it, but when you retire, you're stuck on a fixed income. No more overtime, no more extra details. Thank God I have a wife who's a nurse. Otherwise, I'd probably be sleeping under a bridge somewhere."

"Nah, I don't want to buy it. I was just wondering how often you took it out."

"I get it." He waved his hand between us. "There's no need to work on establishing a rapport. I don't know if you know it or not, but I'm retired law enforcement. You can get right to it. We're already past the rapport building bullshit. Cop to cop, I'm pretty sure I know why you're here."

"Oh, yeah?"

He nodded. "I'm sure you've discovered that I've done some work for Lance, and you're probably hoping I can help you." He paused and frowned. "I'm sorry to tell you, but I can't be of help. His murder came as much of a surprise to me as it did to anyone. I've got no idea who would want him dead."

"Let's start with the work he hired you to do. What did he request of you?"

"Well, you do know that information's privileged. When a client pays me to investigate a case, they own the information I obtain and I can't dispense it without their permission." He shifted in his chair. "I do understand this case is a little unique, considering the client is dead. I don't mind sharing information that I believe will help catch his killer, but I won't reveal things that might compromise him or his reputation. After all, I have my own reputation to maintain."

"Fair enough." I stared him right in the eyes. "Who was he paying you to stalk?"

Francis was a good poker player. He met my stare. "I don't get paid to stalk people. However, I have been paid to conduct surveillance operations. In fact, most of what I do is surveillance. One spouse will suspect the other spouse of cheating and they'll pay me to follow the offending spouse. Sometimes they're right, sometimes they're wrong. Insurance companies pay me to—"

"Lance Beaman wasn't married to Pauline Cain, so why was he paying you to follow her?"

He smiled and the action made his moustache curl up around his nostrils. "Come on, Clint, it's an election year. You know why he was paying me to conduct surveillance on her. Politicians are on their best behavior when they think the cameras are rolling, but if you can catch them when they think no one's looking, well, that's when you find out who they really are."

"And who is Pauline Cain—really?"

Francis took a deep breath. There was a cackling in his chest when he exhaled. "Well, it turns out Pauline Cain is exactly who she pretends to be. Try as I might, I couldn't catch her doing anything wrong. The woman doesn't even spit her gum out the window."

I wanted to sigh in relief, but I didn't respond in any way to what he'd said. And although I was relieved he hadn't found any dirt on my boss, I was still concerned about the lie she'd told me, and I was just a little confused. "That's odd, because Mrs. Beaman said you uncovered evidence that Pauline was sleeping with a married man."

"I don't know why she would say that." He scowled and it was then that I noticed the yellowish stains on the hairs along the bottom of his moustache. "I submitted my report to Lance about a month ago. In it, I clearly detailed everything she did during my surveillance, and that didn't include any adulterous relationships. I'm telling you, the woman's clean as a whistle."

"You'd better quit smoking," I said when he took another deep breath and his chest cackled again. "Those things will kill you."

"I quit two weeks ago. If they're gonna get me, they already have."

"Do you have a lighter?" I asked it as casually as I would ask about the weather. He immediately pushed his chair back and pulled open the top drawer. As he rifled through it for a few seconds, I wondered if he would have had time to shoot at Melvin, run away from him and Amy, somehow escape, and then be back home and cleaned up by the time I knocked on his door.

Finally, he produced a red plastic lighter from the drawer. He handed it to me with a quizzical expression on his face.

"What about an old brass Zippo?"

"God, no." He waved his hand in the air. "I'm always losing lighters, so I buy the cheap ones. Same thing with sunglasses. I'd be sick if I paid a hundred bucks for a lighter or a pair of sunglasses and then lost the damn thing. Remember...*fixed income.*"

We talked briefly about smoking and how much money he was saving since he quit. Since I didn't have a good reason for asking for the lighter and I couldn't make up a convincing one on the fly, I simply plopped it on the desk. I turned the conversation back to the case.

"I'm a bit confused. Mrs. Beaman was positive her husband had information about Pauline sleeping with a married man, and she even said he was going to make that information public if Pauline didn't drop out of the race. If you didn't give him that information, where'd he get it?"

Francis shrugged. "I can't answer that, but I can tell you she was clean. The woman's spotless. If she had been having an affair, trust me, I would've uncovered it."

"How long did you follow her?"

"About six months."

"And you found nothing?"

"Nothing. In fact, I gave him back most of the money he paid me because I felt bad for not finding anything—and for breaking my promise. When we first talked, I assured him I would turn up something embarrassing that he could use. I always do. Look, everyone's got dirt, even Mother Theresa, but"—he shook his head—"Pauline Cain is beyond reproach."

It was my turn to scowl. How on earth would Lance blindly stumble upon that kind of information when Francis had followed her for months and not known anything about it? Did Lance make it up? Was he going to straight up lie about her? I knew lying was not unheard of in politics—in fact, it was more common than not—but who was he going to name as the mystery man?

"Is it possible Lance hired another investigator after you were done?" I asked. "Or maybe Lance began following her himself? How else could he have found out about the affair?"

Francis was a good poker player. His facial expression was like granite and his body language was relaxed, but I detected a telling change to his heart beat. While we'd been talking, I'd noticed his carotid pulse beating at a slow, steady rhythm under the loose skin beside his windpipe. When I asked about the possibility of another private investigator, the skin had jerked violently and his heart was now beating faster. It told me he'd never considered the possibility of another investigator, or the possibility of Lance following Pauline himself, until I mentioned it. This led me to thinking something else.

"So, you gave back some of the money because you felt bad that you didn't produce any results?"

He nodded. "You can ask any of my clients. If I don't feel like I've produced enough results to justify the pay, I usually give them a discount. It's why I keep getting repeat business. Service after the sale…that's a rare thing nowadays."

"You know, Francis, a man gets hired to follow a woman like Pauline…" I let my voice trail off and whistled. "That's a dream assignment."

"It's certainly better than watching some overweight dude swimming laps in a bikini bottom at the Y and waiting to catch him meeting his girlfriend." He leaned back in his chair and nodded for emphasis. "I've had to do that more than once. I don't know how guys who wear bikini bottoms get girls, but I should charge their wives hazard pay for those types of assignments. I swear. I couldn't eat for a week after seeing that crap."

"But watching Pauline in her bikini was a perk, right? Isn't that why you gave back some of the money?"

I noticed a subtle change in his expression. It was almost as though the outer layer of his face was slowly beginning to melt. "No, I gave back the money because I didn't give him information he could use against her. Seeing her in a bikini was lagniappe." He forced a smile and a wink, trying to regain his composure and take command of the conversation.

"Was having sex with her lagniappe, too?" I could almost hear his blood grind to a complete halt in his veins. It took him a half second to process and respond to what I'd just said.

"If you've got something to say, Clint Wolf, why don't you just go ahead and say it?"

"I think Lance knew you fell in love with Pauline. If he hadn't realized it before, he certainly knew it when you returned his money. No one does that unless they feel guilty about something, and you must've felt pretty damn guilty about sleeping with the woman you were paid to expose." I leaned closer, rested my forearms on his desk. "For an investigator and a former cop, you sure got sloppy, though, didn't you? You let an amateur catch you having sex with a mark you were paid to investigate."

"Lance didn't know shit! He was bluffing when he told Pauline he had evidence that she was having an affair. He was trying to use my investigation to scare her into dropping out of the race."

"Is that what Pauline told you?"

"Pauline didn't tell me anything, because we're not having an affair."

"Then how'd you know about the confrontation outside the debate hall?"

"Everyone knows about that."

Everyone didn't know the details like he did, but I decided not to argue that point. I already knew what I needed to know and I knew he wouldn't say more than he already had. Still, I had a couple of more questions for him. "Where were you Sunday evening?"

The sudden change of direction and drop in tone caught him off guard. "Um, I was home. Why?"

"Can your wife verify that?"

He shook his head. "I already told you; she works nights. She leaves at five in the afternoon and gets home at six in the morning. Are you trying to say I killed Lance now? That I was trying to shut him up or something?"

"At the moment, Pauline's a suspect and you're her potential alibi. Either she was somewhere sleeping with you, or she was off killing Lance Beaman. Which is it?"

"How the hell would I know what she was doing? I quit following her when I turned in my report."

"So, are you saying she wasn't with you Sunday night?"

"That's exactly what I'm saying."

"Look, Francis, you and I both know you were sleeping with her. I know you're married and I can promise to try and keep your personal life out of this, but Pauline's facing—at a minimum—life in prison if you don't help establish an alibi for her."

"Are you serious right now?" His brow furrowed. "Are you asking me to lie to protect your boss? Are you trying to coerce me into admitting to an affair I'm not having, just to save your job?"

I stood and smiled down at him. "You have a blessed day."

I dug my phone out of my pocket before I slammed the door behind me, and I was dialing Pauline's number before I'd taken two steps down the driveway. I needed to get her on the phone and keep her there until I could get to the town hall. I didn't want Francis calling her and getting their stories together.

CHAPTER 23

Mechant Loup-North

Susan thanked the K-9 deputy as he walked away and she turned to face Amy, who was still wearing the same clothes from earlier. She had refused to go home and change, saying she wanted to help catch the person who'd tried to kill Melvin. Susan had granted her request because she knew she'd want the same thing if the roles were reversed.

"Well, it looks like the killer got away."

Amy pushed her blonde hair back and crossed her arms, pouting. "I hope Melvin hit him and he's trapped down there at the bottom of the canal."

"Water patrol dragged the entire length of the canal with their grappling hooks. You saw them. They pulled up tree branches, washing machines, old tires, bicycles, and even that dead goat. If he'd been down there, they would've found him." Susan frowned. "Unfortunately, he must've slipped away."

"But how?"

They were still standing near the canal and Susan scanned both banks, from east to west, moving slowly and methodically, trying to figure out how the killer escaped capture. She finally pointed toward the west. "The only way he could've gotten away was if he swam underwater right past us and somehow made it to the highway."

Amy was thoughtful. "You think someone can hold their breath that long?"

"Not the entire distance, but if he quietly came up for air every now and then, it's possible." Susan sighed and turned away from the canal, began the long walk back to North Boulevard. Amy followed, and the two women made their way across the field, then stopped near their vehicles. Susan glanced at the time on her phone. It was almost one o'clock. "Want to grab some lunch before you head home?"

Amy shook her head. "I ate some pizza. The water patrol deputies had three boxes delivered out here. I'll catch some sleep and be back for six."

"Take your time. I'll have Takecia stay out a few extra hours so you can get some rest."

Amy thanked her and started to walk to her car, but stopped and pointed a finger in Susan's direction. "You'd better call me if they spot that—"

"Chief, you out there?" Susan's radio had scratched to life, cutting off Amy.

Susan snatched up the radio. "Go ahead with your traffic, dispatch."

"We just got a call from 311 North Pine. A lady—Mrs. Durapau—said she saw something suspicious this morning, but didn't think anything of it until she just heard about the incident on North Boulevard. She wants to talk to someone about what she saw. Should I dispatch Takecia?"

"Negative!" Susan waved for Amy to follow her. "I'll be there in a minute." Susan jumped in her marked cruiser and sped up the street, across North Main Street, and into the neighborhood on the opposite side of the highway. There was a large culvert under North Main where the drainage canal extended from the Mechant Loup-North subdivision, under North Main, and continued behind the North Pine neighborhood. If the shooter had reached the highway, he could've easily made his way through the culvert and into the other neighborhood.

Susan sped down the street and only slowed when she approached houses. It didn't take her long to reach the three-hundredth-block, and she spotted house number three-eleven right away. "Dispatch, I'm ninety-seven," she said, indicating she had arrived on scene."

Susan waited for Amy to get out of her car and they hurried to the front door together. She glanced sideways at Amy and joked, "Your boyfriend let you out of the house dressed like that?"

Amy glanced down at her mucky uniform and shrugged. "He doesn't want other men to love me, so, yeah."

They laughed while waiting for someone to answer the doorbell.

It didn't take long for the door to swing partly open and for a wide-eyed woman to stick her nose through the crack. "Please, come inside."

Susan stepped back to allow Amy in first. When they were all in the foyer, she had to stifle a chuckle at the expression on Mrs. Durapau's face as she took in Amy's appearance. Amy grinned. "Yes, ma'am, I've had a rough day."

"Oh, dear, my daughter is about your size. She's off at college, but she keeps some clothes here. If you'd like, I can get you a clean pair of jeans and a shirt."

"Thank you, but I'll be fine."

"So, my dispatcher tells me you saw something suspicious this morning."

"Yes, I did." She licked her lips and leaned closer, lowering her voice. "My husband leaves early every morning to go to work. No matter how many times I tell him, he always forgets to put out the garbage. I mean, this has been an ongoing fight for *years*, long before we moved here. Anyway, I was making a pot of coffee when I realized the kitchen garbage was overflowing. The garbage truck passes by here early on Tuesdays and Thursdays, so I hurried and put on my robe and then gathered up all the garbage in the house. I went into the garage and put the bag in the large can."

When the woman paused, Susan nodded patiently, but she wanted to scream, *"Get to it, lady! What did you see?"*

"Once I opened the garage door, I dragged the can to the road and I saw the newspaper sitting there in the street. The lady who delivers the paper never throws it in the driveway. It always ends up in the street, and then it gets trampled by all the cars leaving for work. By the time I get to it, it's usually dirty and rumpled and some of the coupons are too damaged to use. Since I saw it there, I grabbed it before it could get ruined. Thank God my husband didn't run over it as he was leaving."

She stopped, took a breath, and then continued. "As I was about to go back inside, I saw something moving in the field on the western side of my house. It was dark and low to the ground and it was coming from the canal in the back of the property.

"At first I thought it was a coyote, but then I realized it was too long to be a coyote. And then I thought it was an alligator, because we get a lot of those around here, but then I realized it wasn't moving like an alligator. I started to think it might be a giant snake, because I heard people let those big cobras go and they get out in the swamps and grow big—"

"Pythons," Susan corrected.

Mrs. Durapau stopped and cocked her head to the side. "What?"

"We've been having a problem with people releasing their pythons into the wild, not cobras."

"Oh, well, anyway, I realized then that it had to be a man, because when he reached the road, he got to his feet and started walking toward the back of the street, away from my house."

"Are you sure it was a man?" Susan asked.

"Of course I am."

"How can you be sure?"

"I mean, alligators don't stand up and walk, so it had to be a man."

Susan took a breath and smiled. "Could it have been a woman?"

Mrs. Durapau's brow furrowed. "Hmm, I guess that's possible. It just seemed to walk like a man, though."

"Did he see you?" she asked.

"God, I hope not. I don't think so. I stayed in the shadows near the front door and he never looked toward the front of the street that I could tell."

"Did you see where he went?"

She nodded. "He kept walking toward the back of the street and I thought he was heading toward the swamps, but then I saw him cross into someone's yard." She waved for Susan and Amy to follow her outside. She pointed toward the back of the street. "You see that house with the pile of dirt beside the road?"

Susan shaded her eyes from the sun. There was a giant mound of dirt between the street and the house Mrs. Durapau was pointing at, and a portable toilet was situated near a temporary electrical pole. "The one that's under construction?"

Mrs. Durapau nodded. "I saw him cross into that yard. I was about to call the police department when I heard an engine start up. I couldn't see the driveway, but I did see a red glow from the area and I could tell someone was pressing the brakes. I saw the red glow again when a truck pulled out of the yard and headed up the street toward my house. I ducked down behind my bushes right there as he drove by. The funny thing is, he didn't turn on his headlights until he reached the highway."

"And you think it was the same man from the canal?" Susan asked.

"It had to be."

"Did you see him get into the truck?"

She shook her head.

Susan turned her attention to the field beside the woman's house. The grass was short cropped and there were no discernable tracks in the yard that she could see from that distance. "Did you get a good look at him when he drove by your house?"

"Oh, no, I buried my face in the bushes when he drove by. I didn't want him to see me. I'm not trying to get killed out here."

Susan thanked Mrs. Durapau. She and Amy then walked to the street, headed for the field on the western side of the woman's house. They walked along the canal at the back of the lot and located a set of muddy boot prints in the soft mud along the bank of the canal. "Damn, that's him," Susan said. "He made it all the way over here."

Amy stared from the deep boot ruts in the mud to the new construction. "Do you think he called someone to meet him here?"

Susan shook her head. "He probably parked his truck here, walked down the street, then crossed North Main to get to North Boulevard. It's the only way he could've made his way down the boulevard unnoticed." Susan sighed. "Whoever it is, he's smart and allusive."

CHAPTER 24

Mechant Loup Town Hall

"Oh, yeah," I was saying to Pauline on my cell phone as I hurried up the town hall steps and through the front door, "there's a lot of damage to his truck. It might be better to replace it than try to fix it." I smiled and waved to her secretary as I approached her desk. When she realized I wasn't slowing, she opened her mouth and started to stand, but I pointed to my badge and then down at her chair. She clamped her mouth shut and took her seat. Pauline was talking in my ear when I opened the door to her office and stepped inside.

There was a confused expression on her face as her voice trailed off. She glanced down at her cell phone, then slowly placed it on the desk. "I didn't know you were heading this way," she said. "Why didn't you tell me?"

"I wanted to surprise you."

She didn't like the sound of that, but flashed a pleasant smile and pointed to the chair opposite her. "Please, sit."

I did, leaned back and sank into the soft leather. I wiped my face, still trying to decide how to approach her. I'd wrestled with different approaches on the entire drive over here and hadn't settled on one yet. If I took an adversarial tone and accused her of lying, she might shut down and ask for a lawyer. It might also damage our working relationship, and this was something I needed to consider. If she was innocent, she would continue to be my boss and things might be strained between us if I came on too strong. We sat there staring at each other when her phone began to ring.

Before she had time to glance down at the screen, I said, "Don't answer the call. It's Francis Allard."

She tilted her phone so she could see the screen and it appeared that a layer of her tanned face had instantly been peeled away. "How in God's name could you have known that?"

"And I'm sure he was also trying to call you while we were on the phone."

She pressed some buttons on her phone, then stared up at me as though she'd seen a ghost. "How'd you know that?"

I sighed heavily, shifted in my chair. "Look, ma'am, we go way back and I owe you a tremendous debt—"

"I've already told you a hundred times that you owe me nothing."

"Well, I still feel like I do." I drummed my fingers on the desk, still unsure of my next move. If I didn't play this right, I could blow a murder investigation or ruin a perfectly good working relationship. *What the hell?* I thought. *Why don't I just shoot from the hip and see what happens?* "Pauline, you know things don't look good for you."

"How do you mean?"

I wanted to groan out loud. "I mean you're the only one who's got motive to want Lance dead. There's also the issue with the threat that happened out at the debate hall, and then you lied to me about where you were Sunday night."

"Excuse me?"

I leaned closer to her, as though I didn't want my voice to travel beyond the walls of the room, and spoke in a low tone. "Look, if you had nothing to do with Lance's murder, then you're going to continue being the mayor and I'm going to continue working for you. But we have to be able to trust each other. If you lie to me about where you were on Sunday evening, then how I can I trust anything else you tell me? I can't work with someone if I can't trust them."

Pauline's eyes remained fixed on mine. She didn't say a word.

"I already know you've been having an affair with Francis."

What little color she had left completely drained from her face. "How did you find out? Did he tell you?"

I shook my head. "You just did."

She sighed deeply. "Clint, I'm sorry I lied to you, but I couldn't tell you about us. It wasn't my place. He's a married man. He's got so much to lose if his wife finds out, and I wasn't going to be the cause of his problems."

"He's married," I said, "but he's no man."

She cocked her head in a curios angle. "Please explain."

"A real man wouldn't lie to cover his own ass when doing so would jeopardize his girlfriend's freedom. A real man would take a bullet for his girlfriend." I frowned. "I'm sorry to tell you this, but Francis is a coward. I explained to him that if he told the truth about you being with him, it would save you from going to prison for the rest of your life."

"What did he say to that?"

"He accused me of trying to coerce a false confession out of him."

"Did he now?" The color was returning to Pauline's face. "I'm a little surprised. He talked a good game, even said he was going to divorce his wife someday soon. Of course, I wondered why I always had to meet him out at this old boat shed south of town and it had to be when his wife was working. He wasn't taking any chances, that's for sure."

"How long has it been going on between y'all?"

She glanced skyward, moving her lips silently. When she lowered her eyes, she said, "I guess it's been about two months."

"Were you aware that he was working for Lance?"

"Not at first, but he eventually told me. I noticed he would show up everywhere I was and he would always strike up a conversation with me. I was so lonely and didn't really have anything to do and no one with whom to do it. When he started showing an interest in me, well, it felt really good. I felt beautiful and wanted again. That's important to a woman, you know?"

I didn't know, but I nodded and made a mental note to always make Susan feel beautiful and wanted. If she was right and it was important, I wanted to make sure and do it because Susan deserved only my best effort. "I thought you said y'all have been seeing each other for two months?"

"I did."

"Well, Francis said he turned in his report to Lance a month ago."

"Ah, yes. He began feeling guilty for taking his money and sleeping with me, and said something about it probably being unethical, so he quit the case and gave Lance back part of the money."

"Can I ask you a question? It might sound bad."

She hesitated, but then nodded her head.

"Did you start sleeping with him just to influence his investigation into you?"

"Now, there's an idea I wish I could claim." She smiled. "I would've been proud of that one, but the sad truth is I was lonely and I threw myself at the first man who showed a real interest in me. And like I said, I didn't know about the investigation at first."

"How did you feel when he told you he was married? Did you feel used?"

"Maybe I wanted to be used." She shrugged after a moment of reflection. "To be honest, I was probably the one using him. I don't have time for a serious relationship and I figured a married man would be perfect, because I could do what I wanted with him and then send him home to his wife. A man like him—with so much to lose—I knew he wouldn't say a damn thing."

"Did you feel bad for his wife?"

"I know this might sound callous, but I'm not married to his wife. He's the one who made the promise to her, so it's his job to stay faithful. I don't owe that woman anything."

She was right, as it *was* a calloused thing to say, but I kept that thought to myself. "Are you saying you were with him Sunday evening when the murder was committed?"

"I'm not just saying it. It's the truth."

"Do you think he'll verify it?"

She glanced at her cell phone, then up at me. "Let's see…"

I watched as Pauline's thumb danced across the screen and then I heard a phone ringing on her external speaker. It had barely started ringing for the second time when Francis answered. His voice was low. "Pauline? Hey, this is Francis."

"Hey, what's going on?"

"I tried calling you a dozen times."

"Sorry, I was in a meeting. What's up?"

"Did, um, did Clint Wolf stop to see you?"

"Yeah, he stopped by yesterday and asked a bunch of questions about Lance Beaman. I think he believes I killed him."

"What did you tell him?" Francis asked, almost hesitantly.

"I told him that I stayed around the house, went to the grocery store for dinner, then came home and cooked."

"Good, just stick to the truth like that and you'll be fine. If he tries to interview you again, just be cool and don't let him trick you. He'll try to confuse you, so just be careful."

"You're confusing me, Francis." Pauline shot me a wink to let me know she was in control. "I don't understand what this is about. Did he stop by and see you?"

"Yeah, he just came by here. That's why I've been calling. Why didn't you pick up the phone? I must've called twenty times."

"I already told you, I was in a meeting."

"With who?"

"Excuse me?"

"Who was in the meeting?"

"That's none of your business."

His voice got even lower, took on a menacing tone. "What the hell did you just tell me?"

"You heard what I said, Francis Allard. And don't you ever take that tone with me again. Do you understand?"

I thought I'd have to step in and ask her to tone it down, because I wanted Francis to talk to her. If she pissed him off, he might shut down and never talk to her again, but it was apparent she knew what she was doing.

"I'm sorry, Pauline, I'm just a little stressed. If my wife finds out, she'll file for divorce and get half of everything. You know I can't afford for that to happen. I'd lose half my pension."

"I understand, but why didn't you tell Clint you were with me?"

A slight pause. "Why would I say that? I'd never do anything that would jeopardize my marriage, because—"

"I know, I know...you've got a lot to lose. But I could go to prison for the rest of my life. That's a little more serious than some divorce."

Francis scoffed on the other end. "They've got nothing on you. I know how these things work and, trust me, there's nothing for you to worry about."

"I don't want to take that chance. Why don't you just tell them I was with you at the boat shed all night on Sunday and they can move on to the real killer?"

There was a long pause on the other end of the phone. "You lying *bitch!*"

"What is it?" Although Pauline was pretending not to know what he was talking about, her eyes flashed and I was worried she would unleash on him and blow her cover.

"He's there with you, isn't he? Clint Wolf...Clint, are you there? Nice try, detective, but I'm not that stupid."

"No, I'm here," Pauline said in a forceful voice. "I know Clint, and I knew he would find out about our affair. I lied to protect you because I didn't want to be the one to give you away, but I thought you would do the honorable thing and tell him I was with you. Apparently, I was wrong to think you were a real man. You're nothing but a little cheating coward who cares more about himself than anyone else. You certainly don't care about your wife and you don't care about me. And when I called you a little cheating coward, I meant *little!*"

"You know, Pauline, I bet your husband wasn't murdered after all. I bet he killed himself just to be free from you."

Pauline's eyes flashed. "Well, little man, you'll hear it here first; I'm telling Chief of Detective Wolf that I was with you Sunday night and I'm going to give him proof."

"Proof?" Francis let out a contemptuous roar of laughter. "You've got no proof, because it never happened."

"Is that so? Well, how about I give him the old Lynyrd Skynyrd tank top you gave me? I'm betting your wife would recognize that old thing. After all, didn't you say you got it at a concert you attended with her?"

"Try again, sweetheart. There're millions of those shirts around the world."

"Yeah, but only one of them has your DNA all over it. And when your wife realizes yours is missing, it won't take her long to—"

Click.

Pauline lifted an eyebrow. "Well?"

"It's not an admission, but I'm convinced you were with him." I stood to leave, then stopped and stared down at her. "If you had killed Lance, how would you have reacted to the interview Susan and I did with you?"

"I didn't do it, so I don't rightly know." She shrugged. "I guess if I had been guilty, I probably would've fired y'all."

I smiled, pulled out the badge I'd gotten from Sheriff Turner. "Then I guess this was a good move."

She gasped. "Are you quitting?"

"No, it was just a precaution."

She relaxed. "You'd better never leave this town. I don't know what we'd do without you."

I tucked the badge away. "Please don't ever lie to me again. If you ever do, I'll have a hard time staying."

She frowned. "I won't...and I'm sorry."

CHAPTER 25

Mechant Loup Police Department

It was almost four o'clock, and Justin and I had been sitting in my office for about an hour poring over the ledger that listed everyone who had attended Lance Beaman's political event on Sunday. Before leaving for the day, Susan had briefed me about a complaint she'd received earlier where a woman witnessed what appeared to be a man emerging from the canal that linked the neighborhood on the western side of North Main to the eastern side. We'd both agreed it had to be our shooter, and Sheriff Turner had spared two narcotics agents to conduct surveillance on the crime scene in case the killer returned to search for the lighter.

"There're more Detiveauxs than I remembered in this area," Justin said. "I knew there were a lot, but damn, it seems every Detiveaux in Louisiana attended this event."

"That's Beaver Detiveaux's family. They're mad because the former mayor brought me in to replace Beaver years ago." I turned to my desk phone and called the next number on the list. Justin followed suit. I turned to him when I'd finished my call. "Anything?"

He shook his head. "You?"

"Nope. No one knows the name of the guy who refused to sign the ledger and—according to at least two people I spoke with—they weren't allowed to film Lance's speech."

"Makes you wonder what he said in his speech."

I nodded, thoughtful. One lady who remembered the mystery man said he left immediately after Lance's speech and he left through a side door. She never saw him again.

"How's Officer Saltzman?" Justin asked after calling another of the numbers, breaking through my thoughts.

"I think he's struggling a little." I put my copy of the ledger down and looked up at him. "He's a tough cop and he's seen a lot, but there's something about this incident that's got him bothered. I think it was his inability to save Lance. You know yourself that we expect to be able to save people—it's our job—and when we don't, well, I guess he feels like he failed at his job."

Justin stared off in the distance, his brow furrowing a bit. Finally, he looked back in my direction. "I think you heard me telling Officer Saltzman about the kid I wasn't able to save."

I nodded.

"It wasn't the first. But when it happened again, I was so filled with self-hatred that I almost killed myself." He paused, the corner of one eye twitching a little. "You know what helped me the most and what might be able to help your officer?"

"What's that?"

"I don't know if you're aware of this, but there's this tri-parish support group made up of police officers and fire fighters who've been through similar things. There are a couple of deputies from the sheriff's office who are members, along with some fire fighters from the volunteer company I used to run with back in the day. In fact, Ox Plater and a few paramedics I know are also members."

I'd heard of the group. While I preferred to deal with my own baggage privately, I knew they did good work and that many people responded well to that type of therapy. I agreed when Justin said it might be beneficial for Melvin to check it out.

"They usually meet on the third Thursday of every month," Justin said, "but when there's a first responder in crisis, they call an emergency session. This would qualify as an emergency. I don't go anymore since I moved out of town, but if your officer is willing, I can call Ox to get the ball rolling. They can usually throw a meeting together within twenty-four hours."

I figured it might be easier for Melvin to speak with his peers— those first responders who had experienced similar tragedies—about what he was experiencing rather than a counselor, so I stepped out into the hallway to give him a call while Justin contacted Ox.

"I don't know, Clint," Melvin said when I pitched the idea to him. "I'm not thrilled about sitting in a circle and pouring out my feelings to complete strangers."

"I wouldn't do it," I said plainly.

Melvin laughed. "Damn, are trying to talk me into it or out of it?"

"Neither. I just want you to be okay, so whatever you need..."

"I appreciate you caring about me." He was silent for a long moment. "I'll do it. When's the first meeting?"

"Hold on." I stuck my head in my office. "Well?"

"Tonight, seven-thirty," Justin said. "Ox has six people already committed to showing up and someone's bringing pizza, so tell him to bring an empty stomach."

I passed along the message and Melvin thanked me before hanging up. When I walked back into my office, Justin tossed his copies of the ledger toward me.

"I'm all done," he said. "No one seems to know who this joker is and I've got at least four different descriptions of him. One man said he was short and skinny with blond hair, another woman said he was medium height and had dark hair, while someone else said he was bald."

I scowled as I studied the names on the list. "Someone has to know something about this guy."

I looked up when I noticed Justin staring at me. "Are you sure it's not your boss?" he asked.

"Positive."

"But how can you be so sure? She's the only one with motive to want the man dead."

"She's got a solid alibi."

"But what if her alibi witness is in on it, too?" Justin leaned back in his chair and kicked his boots up on my desk. "After all, didn't he deny being with her at first?"

"He did, but that was because he didn't want his wife finding out about the affair."

"And how'd you convince him to admit that he was banging the mayor if he didn't want his wife to know about it?"

I smiled as I described the look on Francis' face when I showed up at his front door carrying the Lynyrd Skynyrd tank-top he had given Pauline. "Has your old ass ever heard of Facebook?"

Justin grunted. "I've got four children and eight grandchildren— what do you think? According to one of my grandchildren, Facebook is for people just like me—old and not cool."

"Well, Francis posted a picture of him wearing that tank-top on Facebook and there was a stain on the left shoulder strap. Since he was a homicide detective in his first life, he recognized the effectiveness of pattern analysis and he knew I could prove the shirt I was holding in my hand was the same one he had been wearing in that picture." I nodded smugly. "I gave him two choices; he could either tell me the truth, or I could get on my bullhorn and wake up his wife so she could identify his shirt. I told him she probably didn't wear the same kind of perfume that was all over the fabric."

"Pretty slick, but what if he told you what you wanted to hear just to protect his marriage?"

"I always consider that," I explained, "so I made him give me details about his evening with Pauline—details only he and Pauline would know—to convince me. He passed the test. He actually told me more than I wanted to know. I'll never be able to look her in the eye again."

"What if they got their stories straight before you interviewed him?"

I shrugged. "The devil is definitely in the details, and no two criminals will ever think of every question we'll ask."

Justin took a deep breath and blew it out forcefully. "Well, if Pauline isn't the killer, then this mystery man will be our next best guess, but we can't even figure out who the hell he is."

"Maybe tomorrow will bring more luck." I glanced at the clock on my computer monitor. "Let's grab some dinner, my treat. Then we'll have to get some sleep while we can. Once this thing breaks, we could be running and gunning for days."

CHAPTER 26

Center Chateau Parish Volunteer Fire Station

Melvin licked his lips, sat in his truck for a while, and stared at the other vehicles in the parking lot. Claire had been supportive and even pleased that he'd agreed to seek help for what was troubling him, but he was starting to have doubts. *What if I go to the park instead for a couple of hours and call it even?*

The thought was enticing, but then he'd have to lie to Claire if she started asking questions, and he didn't want to lie to his wife. Headlights splashed against him as another car pulled into the driveway. Feeling as though he'd been busted doing something wrong, he shut off the engine and stepped outside.

"Melvin!" The person in the other car hurried around her vehicle and ran up to him, throwing her arms around his neck for a quick hug.

When she pulled back, Melvin cocked his head to the side. "Stephanie?"

She raised her hands into the air. "Guilty as charged!"

Melvin had to rub his eyes. He had met Stephanie years ago when she covered the Mechant Loup area for the Chateau Ambulance Service. He'd seen her many times since then, but he hadn't recognized her outside of uniform when she first walked up. It was amazing how different a woman could look with her hair down, wearing a short skirt, blouse, and sandals versus sporting a bun and wearing polyester greens.

"What are you doing here?" she asked.

Melvin scowled. "I'm the reason for the special session."

"And let me guess…you were sitting in your truck thinking about driving out of here as fast as you could."

He turned his head from side to side, scanning the parking lot, then looked back at her. "How on earth would you know that? Do you have my truck bugged or something?"

She placed a soft hand on his forearm. "I've been there. I was terrified when I came to my first meeting, and that was six years ago. I've conquered my fears and now I come here to help others conquer theirs."

Melvin stared down at Stephanie. Her brown hair was hanging free and her brown eyes sparkled with joy. He wanted to feel joy again…wanted everything to go back to normal. While he'd managed to eat lunch earlier in the day, he still smelled Lance's burnt flesh from time to time. He sighed, indicated with his hand toward the entrance to the volunteer fire department. "Ladies first."

Stephanie bounded in front of him and he wondered why she was there. Whatever the reason, it must've really helped, because she sure seemed at peace.

When he pulled the door open for her, he immediately took in the room and knew the layout before he committed to stepping inside. He'd been here before. Every now and then the police department would put on trainings for the fire department, addressing subjects such as report writing, courtroom testimony, and evidence preservation, while the fire department certified the officers in first aid, CPR, and fire prevention.

There were seven people there besides him—four men and three women. Other than Stephanie, he only recognized Ox Plater and a deputy from the Chateau Parish Sheriff's Office. Each member walked up to him intermittently within the first ten or so minutes he was there and offered a casual introduction. They weren't trying to smother him and they weren't overly friendly. No one asked why he was there. Instead, they made casual talk about current events, the possibilities of the Saints winning a second Super Bowl in the upcoming season, and whether he preferred pepperoni or supreme pizza. It felt as though he was attending a regular training session rather than seeking help, and he liked it. It made him feel more at ease about being there.

After a bit, a man in a shirt and tie asked everyone if they were ready to start the meeting. After a chorus of nods, everyone gravitated toward the circle of chairs at the front of the room. There were fifteen chairs, so most of the members sat with an empty chair between them. Stephanie took a seat next to Melvin, and he couldn't help but wonder if they'd assigned her to be his sponsor, or spy, or whatever it was called for this type of support group.

"We've got a new member with us tonight," the man said, "so let's all take turns telling him a little about ourselves and why we're here. I'll begin."

After the man with the suit was done, another man stood up and introduced himself, then talked about a shooting that happened one night when he was working patrol with the sheriff's office. His partner had been shot and he tried to save her, but she died in his arms. Now a detective, the man still had trouble working with a partner because he was afraid he would fail them like he had failed his patrol partner.

Ox went next and, although Melvin could tell he was trying to avoid making eye contact with him, he kept glancing in Melvin's direction.

"When I was a young fireman, I responded to a crash one night. It was to be my first crash with injuries. I'd already been on the job for a couple of years and I'd been to countless trainings, but nothing prepared me for what I would see that night." Ox paused and swallowed hard. His eyes were misty and Melvin thought he would start crying. "Some drunk driver in a pickup truck hit a minivan one night. The occupants were trapped inside and the van burst into flames. When I arrived I was in my POV (personally owned vehicle) and I didn't have my gear. I tried desperately to save them, but—" Ox lowered his head and squeezed the bridge of his nose between the thumb and index finger of his left hand. When he continued detailing the horrors he faced that night, his voice crackled and he had to stop several times to summon the strength to go on.

Melvin stared in awe. He'd been involved in a number of high-stress situations with Ox and had never seen the man so emotional. He'd never heard Ox's real name called and always guessed he had earned the nickname from being tough as an ox.

"I wasn't able to save them and they burned to death in that van." He shook his head. "It was horrible. No matter how many times I tell that story and how many years have passed, I still get choked up. But"—he waved his hand around the circle of chairs—"thanks to the founding members of this group, I've been able to come to terms with the events of that night and I was able to recognize early on that we are all human and there are limits to what we can do.

"As long as we do our best and give our all, we can put our heads on the pillow each and every night and sleep soundly, knowing we've done God's work. It won't always be easy and we're sure to face trials and tribulations along the way, but, if we stick together and encourage one another as we have for the past several years, we can find a way to survive emotionally.

"I've said it before and I'll say it again, if you walk away from the job in one piece but you're an emotional wreck inside, you're not a survivor—you're a time bomb waiting to go off."

Ox turned his head from left to right, then handed the microphone to the person on his left to keep it going in the same direction.

When the microphone reached Melvin, he took it and handed it to Stephanie without saying a word. He expected an objection from someone, but no one seemed to notice.

Stephanie stood immediately to her feet and talked about a call she had answered about a toddler drowning in a swimming pool.

"I'd practiced CPR on dummies a million times up to that point," she recounted, "but it was the first time I had to perform it on a real person. When I saw how small the child was, I panicked. I couldn't remember what to do. People were screaming at me to do something. The mother was begging me to help her child. I spent the first fifteen or twenty seconds just staring at the toddler. She couldn't have been more than two years old. I had a niece that age and I kept seeing her face as I stared down. By the time I got it together and started working on the baby, it was too late."

She frowned and stared down at her feet. "Although the emergency room doctor told me the baby was already too far gone and I couldn't have saved her even if I had started CPR immediately, I still blamed myself for her death."

Melvin sat in his chair feeling despondent. Twenty minutes ago Stephanie was jovial and didn't seem to have a care in the world, yet here she was looking like she was about to break down.

He began to feel more uncertain about attending these meetings. *If I were to finally get over my situation, why would I come here once a month just to relive it and get all depressed again?*

He made a mental note to pose that question to Stephanie when this was over. He didn't have to wait long. About fifteen minutes later the last person had told her story and they concluded the sharing portion of the meeting. Next, everyone got in line for a slice or two of pizza and a cold drink. Melvin swallowed hard, took a plate with one piece and followed Stephanie to one end of the tables that were situated to the back of the room. He sat across from her.

"Hey, can I ask you a question?" he asked.

"Sure." She popped the top off a can of soda and poured it in a plastic cup. "Ask away."

"You were in a good mood when you walked in, but then you told that story and everything seemed to change. You looked sad and depressed."

She nodded slowly. "Yes…"

"So, why would you come here every month and tell your story?"

"I don't come here every month and tell my story." She smiled warmly. "I told that story for you. I wanted you to know what I've been through so you would know you're not alone."

Melvin picked at his pizza with a plastic fork, trying not to look at it. He didn't know what to say. Finally, he asked, "Why'd you do it if it hurt you?"

"It's therapy for me," she explained simply. "Every time I tell the story, I cry a little less. I'm hoping someday I can talk about it without crying at all."

"You seemed so happy when I first saw you tonight."

"That's because I was."

"But how can you be so happy if you've got that weight in the back of your mind?"

Stephanie gave Melvin a knowing look. "After a while, you'll go from thinking about it every second to every minute. And then, after a while longer, you might think about it every couple of hours. As you put more time and distance between you and the situation, you'll go days and even months without thinking about it. For me, I only get sad now when I hear or see something that triggers a memory of that night, or when I come to these meetings and share my story."

Melvin thought his pizza looked too much like Lance Beaman's burnt body, so he pushed the plate aside. "How did you make it through those first few days?" he asked. "How were you able to deal with it until you reached the point of not thinking about it every second of every day?"

Stephanie looked around to make sure no one was in earshot, then leaned across the table until her face was inches from Melvin's. "A wise person once told me you have to imagine the victim did something so horrible that they deserved what happened to them."

Melvin lurched backward. "Wait…what? Who in the hell would do something like that?"

"Not so loud!" Stephanie hissed. "Look, I know it's not a popular method of coping, but if you imagine Lance Beaman did something so horrible in his past life that he deserved to be burned alive, it'll help you get through the initial pain."

Melvin sat there trying to process what she'd just told him. "So, all I have to do is imagine Lance Beaman deserved to be burned alive and it'll help ease whatever it is I'm feeling?"

"Yes, but you can't just *imagine* it," she warned. "You have to *believe* it."

He studied the sweet woman in front of him. She scared him. "Did you do that with your victim? I mean, what on earth could a two-year-old child do that would warrant being drowned to death?"

Stephanie sighed, her eyes clouding over. "It's amazing what your mind will make you believe when it's trying to heal itself."

CHAPTER 27

Wednesday, April 26
Mechant Loup Police Department, Southeast Louisiana

"We've been through every name on this list—some of them twice," Justin was saying, "and no one knows the mystery guest."

I was leaning back in my chair with my feet on the desk scanning the names on the list one last time. When I was done, I glanced over at Justin. We had been in my office since eight o'clock—over an hour—and we hadn't gotten anywhere. I was starting to wonder if we were wasting our time searching for this mystery guest. "Did you hear back from the crime lab?"

He shook his head, stood to his feet. "I'll call them after I use the little boy's room."

I dropped my feet heavily to the floor and sat with my elbows on the desktop, drumming my fingers as I went over everything we'd done so far. As evidence went, there wasn't much to go on. Even if the lighter produced evidence that led us to an individual, we couldn't definitively tie it to the murder. There was always the possibility it was thrown from a vehicle or someone dropped it while cutting grass along the boulevard. "That's what I'd say anyway," I said out loud.

"What would you say?"

I looked up to see Susan leaning against the doorway. Her arms were folded in front of her and the muscles in her upper arms stretched the sleeves of her tan uniform shirt. I waved dismissively. "I was just talking to myself."

"You do that a lot. I'm starting to think you're older than you let on." She sauntered over and sat on the corner of my desk, stared down at me. "I'm guessing it's not going so great?"

"We haven't gotten anywhere with the ledger. No one seems to know this stranger."

"Find the motive, find the—"

"God, I'm starting to regret saying that." I shook my head. "The motive for this one could be anything."

"The most obvious reason for wanting him dead is the election, wouldn't you say?"

I nodded.

"And your prime suspects would be Pauline Cain and Zack Pitre, correct?"

I nodded again, then added, "But they each have alibi witnesses who put them elsewhere at the time of the murder."

"Sure, but, other than the two candidates themselves, who has the most to lose if they don't win the election?"

I studied Susan for a full minute before answering. "As far as I know, no one in Zack's camp would lose anything if he didn't become mayor, but Pauline is a different story."

"Exactly!" Susan stabbed a finger in my chest. "So start looking at those people close to Pauline." My expression must've been blank, because Susan cocked her head to the side. "What's wrong?"

"You and I have the most to lose if Pauline doesn't win, so I guess we'll have to start right here."

"That's nonsense. We can each verify that we were home together when we got the call."

"No one would believe that. They'd believe we were covering for each other because we were both in on it."

"You're missing the point entirely." Susan placed her cool hands on either side of my face and moved forward until her nose was inches from mine. "Think about it...if this mystery guest killed Lance, then he has to support Pauline or Zack. Go to them and see if the description matches someone they know; someone close to them."

My eyes widened. "That's a brilliant idea!"

"I'm good, aren't I?" Her face lighting up, she playfully kissed my forehead and strutted out of my office. Before she disappeared around the doorway, she called over her shoulder, "I was trained by the best."

"Nope. That was all you," I said under my breath as I snatched the handset from its cradle. I dialed the town hall and asked for Mayor Cain. She picked up in a hurry.

"Hey, Clint, how'd it go with Francis? Did he verify we were together?"

"Yeah, he did."

There was an audible sigh from the other end. "Thank God. I told you so."

"We might have another problem, though."

"Oh no, what's that?" Her voice betrayed the angst she suddenly felt.

"We're looking for someone who might serve on your campaign committee. It would be a white male, well-groomed, and he wears a fancy suit."

She let out a nervous laugh. "You've just described half the men on my campaign."

"Do they all wear red ties?"

Pauline sucked in her breath and my ears perked up. "Oh, dear," she said in a low voice, "you don't think what I think you're thinking, do you?"

"And what's that?"

"This man who wears the red tie…why are you looking for him? You don't suppose he's involved with Lance's murder, do you?"

"Hey, Clint, I just got off the phone with the lab—"

I quickly waved at Justin, who had burst into my office, to let him know I was in the middle of something. He abruptly stopped walking and talking, then approached me quietly.

"We don't know for sure," I said. "All we know is that someone fitting that description went to Lance's campaign event on Sunday. Do you know someone who matches?"

Pauline paused for a long moment. "Clint, it's impossible. There's no way he would've done something like this. He's loyal to me, yes, and that is exactly why he would never have done anything like this. He would've known it would reflect poorly on me, so he would never have done it."

"Who are we talking about?"

"I think you already know."

Although she couldn't see me, my eyes widened. "You're right, I do know."

CHAPTER 28

"Who is it?" Justin whispered as I continued speaking with Pauline.

"Please, Clint," Pauline said on the other end of the phone, "you've got to promise me he never knows I said his name. I don't want him thinking I betrayed him or that I suspected him of doing anything like this, because I know better."

"You didn't say his name. I figured it out, but he'll never know we had this conversation. The only thing I need from you is a picture so I can prepare a photographic lineup. If someone at the party can identify him, then I can leave you out of it completely."

"Picture?" she asked. "What kind of picture?"

"A frontal face shot, something similar to a passport photo."

"I have some pictures on my website, but they're from campaign events. They're not professionally done. You could easily find those yourself if you would simply view my website."

I slid my chair toward my computer and started typing in the name of her website. When the home page popped up, I asked where to find the picture.

"Go to the *Appearances* page," she said, "and scroll through the pictures. I can't log in to my campaign site from work, so I can't tell you exactly where he is on the page, but there are a bunch of pictures of him. He's with me at every event."

"Was he with you on Sunday?"

"No. I spoke to him early Sunday morning, but he didn't say anything about attending Lance's event."

"Did he know about your affair with Francis?"

Pauline was silent, then said in a low voice, "No."

I thanked her and was about to hang up when she stopped me. "Please go easy on him. I know he had nothing to do with this, so I hope you won't interrogate him and make him feel like he's being accused of any wrongdoing. He's been really good to me and I don't want—"

"It'll be fine." I ended the call and clicked on a picture of the man standing all alone at one of Pauline's events, near a table of finger food.

Justin was hovering over me now and he leaned forward and squinted to read the caption. "Who in the hell is Stephen Butler?"

"He used to work for Hays and Pauline Cain out at their house," I explained. "Pauline let him go not long after her husband's murder, but, from what I understand, he'll never have to work another day in his life."

Justin grunted. "If he killed Lance Beaman, he'll be doing hard labor for the rest of his life."

I only nodded as I cropped his head out of the photo and saved it to a file. I searched through the other events and found a better photo of him. It looked more like a mug shot, but without the prison uniform. As I began searching our electronic databank of prisoners, I asked Justin about the call he received from the lab.

"Oh, yeah, they recovered a fingerprint from the lid of the lighter, and they also swabbed the flint wheel for DNA. They ran the print through AFIS (Automated Fingerprint Identification System), but they didn't get a hit. They're still working on the DNA."

"What about the glass from the murder scene and the samples of accelerant?"

He smiled and exposed a row of pearly whites. "What did I tell you? That test only confirmed what my nose already knew." He started to spout some technical terms, but I stopped him.

"Consider your audience," I said. "Keep it simple."

"Gasoline and motor oil. The glass was thick and green, probably from an old soda bottle."

"That narrows it down to the millions." I stopped what I was doing to consider the evidence. "What about the shell casings? Did they run them through IBIS (Integrated Ballistics Identification System)?"

He nodded. "Nothing."

"God, I hope Stephen Butler either did it or leads us to the one who did, because if he didn't or doesn't, we're screwed."

Justin took a seat beside me and watched as I worked on the photo lineup. Neither of us said much of anything as I used the drawing program we'd purchased two years ago to create the same kind of outfit for each of the six men in my photo spread. Once I was satisfied, I printed the document in color on photo paper and handed it to Justin. "What do you think?"

"Number Two did it."

"Is it that obvious?" I studied each man's mug to make sure they appeared fair. While the other photographs were of prisoners and Stephen's was from a social setting, I thought I'd done a decent job of disguising that fact.

"Nah, I just know a guilty bastard when I see one."

I grunted. "They're all guilty— unless you believe the others were wrongfully arrested and convicted."

"Well, Number Two has the eyes of an arsonist. Look at him. You can see the devil in those eyes."

I leaned close, shook my head. "My devil vision must be blurry, because I don't see anything."

I slipped the photo lineup in a file folder and gave Chet Robichaux a call. As I'd expected from any retired man, he was cutting his grass and invited me to meet him in his driveway. "I might even put you to work," he said. "I've got a cypress stump that needs to come out of the ground and I could use the extra muscle."

I just laughed and asked Justin if he was ready to go.

"Yeah, it's time we put this thing to rest. My boss has been calling me nearly every hour to find out if it's solved yet."

While I had mixed feelings about Stephen being the killer, I wanted the case solved, too. Justin shook his head when I drove by the scarred concrete along North Boulevard and then turned into Chet's driveway. "I can't believe it's only been three days since the murder. It seems like a month ago that I met you out here."

I nodded, stepped from my Tahoe and approached Chet. He had parked his blue tractor at the edge of his driveway and slid off the seat. He looked a lot older in faded jeans and a flannel shirt. He pulled off a leather glove and shook our hands. "Want some lemonade?"

Justin and I both declined. "I've got some pictures for you to look at," I explained. "We may or may not have found the stranger from your meet-and-greet. We need you to look at a picture spread and see if you recognize any of the men in the lineup."

"Is he definitely in one of the pictures?" Chet shoved his gloves in a back pocket and pulled some reading glasses from his shirt pocket.

"We don't know," I said. "Only you can tell us if he is."

He nodded and licked his lips as I opened the file folder and pulled out the picture spread. All of the names had been removed from the photos and all that remained were the pictures and corresponding numbers from one through six. I handed it to him. "Take your time and—"

"It's him!" Chet stabbed a thin finger over Stephen Butler's face. "That's the little bastard who was at the event!"

I knew I didn't have to, but I asked if he was positive.

"As sure as the Louisiana sun is hot, that's the man who came to Lance's meet-and-greet!"

I pursed my lips, thanked him.

"Are you going to arrest him?"

"We don't know if he did anything wrong, so I can't answer that question just yet."

"Huh, I know he did it!"

Once we were back in my Tahoe, I fielded a call from Mrs. Beaman, who wanted to know what was taking so long to catch her husband's killer. I apologized and tried to explain the investigative process, but she was having none of it.

"I've got a news van over here interviewing me, and I'm going to tell them how you're in the bag for Pauline if I don't get some answers—and get them quick!" She hung up before I could say anything, which was probably best. I had a way of saying things that pissed people off at times, so she most likely saved me from myself.

"Where are we heading?" Justin asked.

"Stephen lives in the back of town. I think it's time we pay him a visit."

Justin's face was beaming. "That's what I'm talking about! Let's take this bastard down!"

I called Susan and let her know where we were going.

"Do y'all want some backup?" she asked. "I'm around the corner."

"Sure," I said. "We could use someone to cover the back."

"I'll round up Baylor and we'll meet y'all near the east bridge."

I ended the call, sped across town, down Washington Avenue, and then took a left onto the bridge that connected the west side of town with the east side. Susan was parked on the shoulder of the road and Baylor's marked cruiser was next to her vehicle. They fell in behind us as we crossed the bridge and turned on to East Holy Street. Stephen's house was at the corner of Holy and Cypress Highway.

While the house was small and aged, there was a long tract of wooded land behind it, and it had all been signed over to him by

Pauline. It was prime deer-hunting property, and the back of his property pushed up against the small canal that connected Bayou Tail with Forbidden Bayou. Since no one spent much time back there, I'd heard the canal was overflowing with massive bass, hubcap-sized perch, and catfish that were too big for most alligators to eat.

"There he is!" Justin pointed to the front yard, where Stephen was kneeling with his back to the street, elbow-deep in his flowerbed.

Susan overtook me and passed me up, turning the corner to cover the eastern side of Stephen's house. I parked directly in front, which was to the south, and quickly stepped out. Justin's feet hit the pavement a second behind mine. Stephen whirled around when he heard the doors slam and I saw a spade in his right hand.

"Drop that tool or I'll drop you!" Justin hollered, his pistol pushed out in front of him as he led the way toward Stephen.

CHAPTER 29

"What on earth is going on?" Stephen immediately dropped the tool and Justin slowed to a stop about thirty feet from him.

My pistol was still holstered, as was Susan's. I stepped forward and gave Justin a nod to let him know I was going in to talk with Stephen. Justin lowered his weapon, but didn't holster it. I had a feeling that if Stephen even let out a sneeze Justin would send an army of hot lead in his direction.

"Why was he pointing a firearm at me?" Stephen asked when I reached him. "And why is my yard surrounded by police cars?"

"I need to ask you some questions about Lance Beaman," I explained. "I know you were at his political event Sunday, right before he was murdered."

"Well, I did not murder him, if that is what you are wondering."

"It is what I'm wondering." I shot a thumb toward my Tahoe. "Do you mind coming for a ride with me?"

"As a matter of fact, I do mind." He shot a hard stare in Justin's direction. "I was just assaulted by that man, so I am not feeling very inspired to honor your request."

"I apologize for that, but I'm sure you must've heard about the attack on Officer Melvin Saltzman." I leaned closer. "It's got everyone on edge, if you know what I mean. Anytime someone makes an attempt on a cop's life, well, it inspires other cops to be a little more cautious."

Stephen pursed his lips. "I can appreciate that, but I know I did not do anything wrong, so I do not feel like I have to accompany you to your office. If you would like to come inside, I would be happy to answer any questions you might have."

"That would be great." I stepped forward and Justin started to follow me.

"Not you, sir." Stephen shook his head. "You nearly took my life, so I do not want you in my home."

"What about me?" Susan asked. "Is it okay if I come inside?"

Stephen's face softened. "You are always welcome in my home."

I nodded to let Justin know it was okay. He begrudgingly shoved his pistol in its holster and ambled toward Baylor Rice's cruiser. "I wished he hadn't dropped that tool," I heard him say to Baylor, who only stared after Susan and me.

When we were inside, Stephen led us through the kitchen and he stopped at the sink to wash his hands. "Please, have a seat."

I dropped in a chair at the head of the table and shifted it so my back was to the wall and I could scan the entire room. Susan took up a chair to my right and I noticed she kept her hand close to her pistol.

"Do you mind telling me what led you to attend Lance's political event?" I asked when Stephen had dropped to a chair across from Susan.

"Opposition research," he said simply. "I wanted to know what he was saying about Mrs. Cain and I wanted to hear his plans for the future of our town."

"I take it you were alone?"

He nodded.

"What time did you leave?"

"I did not look at my watch, but it was toward the end of the speech. I slipped out a side door and left before anyone could figure out who I was. I did what I did of my own accord and Mayor Cain knew nothing about it."

"And when you say you *did what you did*, do you mean you—"

"I am referring to my attendance at the rally, nothing more. Mayor Cain did not know I was conducting opposition research, and I intend to keep it that way." He frowned. "I guess it does not matter any longer."

"Yeah, the only real competition she had is frozen in the morgue at the moment, and he ain't coming back." I rubbed my face. "Where'd you go when you left the event?"

"I walked to where my car was parked and drove away. I stopped at Cig's for a pound of luncheon meat, bread, and a bottle of wine. Next, I drove home and made myself a sandwich." He spread his hands palms-down across the table. "Is there anything else you would like to know?"

"What time did you get home?"

"It must have been around seven-thirty when I arrived. After I ate my sandwich, I put out some feed for the neighborhood cats and then I sat down to watch television."

"Do you remember what you watched?"

He shook his head. "The Walking Dead had its season finale at the beginning of the month, so I have no idea what I watched. I most likely flipped through the channels until about nine o'clock, at which time I would have retired to my bedroom for the night."

I glanced around the tiny kitchen. "Do you live here alone?"

"Yes, I do."

"So, no one can confirm your whereabouts Sunday night, right?"

"Sure, I can confirm where I was Sunday night."

"I'm looking for an independent witness who can corroborate your statement," I explained. "Otherwise, all I have is your own self-serving statement."

"Well, then, I guess you will have to settle for my self-serving statement, because that is all I have to offer."

I studied the man's face carefully, searching for the slightest hints of a lie. I didn't detect any, but that didn't mean they weren't there. "You're loyal to Mayor Cain, aren't you?"

"Most certainly."

"And I'm guessing you would do anything for her, right?"

"Absolutely."

"Would you kill for her?"

"I would."

I stifled a grin of admiration. Most people wouldn't admit they'd kill for someone, especially when they were the potential target of a murder investigation. "And how do you feel about Lance being dead?"

The right corner of his mouth curled up just a little. "Quite pleased, actually. The man was going around saying some vile things about Mrs. Cain." He shrugged. "I feel it was just."

I spent another five minutes, or so, asking more questions, but I was no closer to figuring out for sure if he did it or not.

"Does the name Francis Allard mean anything to you?"

There was a subtle shift of Stephen's eyes, almost indiscernible, but I'd noticed.

"I might have heard the name before," was all he said.

"Were you aware that Pauline was having an affair?"

Stephen slammed his fist on the table. "How dare you perpetuate the rumors that Lance Beaman started about Mrs. Cain!"

I didn't flinch and my expression remained fixed. "Save the

drama, Stephen. I already know about the affair."

Where there had been fire in his eyes a split-second earlier, there was now doubt. His eyes drifted from me to Susan, who nodded solemnly. He lowered his head and his voice was low. "That kind of thing could derail her campaign. I tried to advise her to stop seeing the man, but I believe she cares for him. I did not want to say this to her, but I believe he is using her. He is not good for her and she deserves much better."

As I studied Stephen's body language while he talked about Pauline, I made a mental note to arrest him immediately if Francis ever turned up dead.

"How'd you know about the affair?" I asked.

"As a loyal supporter of Mrs. Cain, I took it upon myself to keep an eye on her when I could. A lady like her, a widow who lives alone, she needs someone to look after her."

"You've been following her?"

He hesitated. "It was only once or twice, when I would encounter her along the highway, and I only did it to keep her safe."

"Am I correct in assuming you caught her with Francis?"

"I had gone to the grocery store late one night right before they closed. As I was pulling out of the parking lot, I saw Mrs. Cain drive by. She was heading south, which I thought was odd. I decided to follow her to make sure she was not in distress.

"As I was following behind her, she drove to an old boat shed she used to own that is south of town. It is where Mr. Cain used to keep one of his boats. When she arrived, there was already another car in the parking lot and I was a little concerned, but I remained in hiding. I waited until she went inside and then I made my way to the back window and peered inside."

His hands began to tremble and he shoved them in his lap and out of view. "There is a kitchen and a bedroom in the boat shed, and this strange man was preparing a meal over the stove. When he was finished, they ate together and then disappeared in the bedroom. I waited on the shoulder of the road until they left, and I followed the man home. That is when I realized the identity of the man."

"Did you continue following her?"

He shook his head. "I should have, but I did not like what I saw and I did not want to see it again."

I detected real pain and anger in Stephen's voice, and I knew he was in love with Pauline. Hell, half the men in this town were in love with her. "Did you confront her about the affair?"

"Not at first, but I did when she told me about the threat Lance had made."

"As a loyal supporter, didn't you want to retaliate against Lance for making a threat against Pauline?"

"I did."

"And did you?"

"I did not."

"You expect me to believe you sat idly by while this man was threatening the woman you love?"

Stephen looked up for a long moment, focusing on some spot in the ceiling. When he spoke, his voice trembled. "I cut his brake lines."

I nearly choked on my tongue. "You did *what?*"

The man sighed heavily and his shoulders slumped. "I slipped out of the event before anyone else and made my way to his vehicle. I looked carefully around. When I was sure there were no witnesses, I severed the brakes lines near all four tires. I did want him to die for what he had done to Mrs. Cain, but I did not cause his death. Someone else beat me to it."

"I need you to think very carefully…did you hear or see anything at all when you were cutting his brake lines?"

"No."

"Any movement or noise from that clump of trees located at the center of the boulevard?"

"Nothing."

I nodded, began pressing him further on what he'd already said, asking pointed questions and rephrasing them to be sure he was telling the truth. I couldn't get him to contradict anything he'd already said. Either he was that good at lying or he didn't kill Lance. When I was done, I surveyed the room. "Do you mind if I search your house?"

"For what?"

"A nine millimeter pistol."

"I do not own any weapons."

"Is that a yes or a no?"

He waved his hand around. "Help yourself."

Susan and I spent the next hour searching for a pistol. We touched everything in sight—moved boxes, opened drawers, checked pockets of clothes—but didn't turn up a weapon. When we were done, we followed Stephen back to the kitchen and he sank back to his chair at the kitchen table. I was thoughtful as I studied him, trying to see through to his very soul, searching for any hint that he might be the one responsible for killing Lance. "You know you can go to jail for what you did, don't you?"

He nodded, sighed. "And I am prepared to do so, but I do not want it known that I am an associate of Mrs. Cain's. I do not want my actions to reflect poorly on her campaign."

It was my turn to sigh. "Well, considering the victim hasn't filed a complaint about the cut brake lines and it didn't cause his death, I guess there isn't much we can do about that now."

Besides, I thought, *the brake lines have been completely destroyed by the fire, so all we have is your uncorroborated confession.*

"I just want you to know one thing; I'm not convinced you didn't kill Lance, but if you did, and if you're the one who shot at Melvin, I'm going to find out about it and I'll be back for you—and I won't be as nice as I was today."

He simply nodded and remained seated while Susan and I turned and walked out of his house.

CHAPTER 30

"What the hell happened in there?" Justin asked. "Y'all were inside so long I was about to call out the SWAT team."

I explained what Stephen had told us, and Justin scowled. "He admitted to cutting the brake lines?"

"Yep."

"Then he burned the man alive!" He pointed back toward the house. "We need to drag him into the station and interrogate the hell out of him."

"We can't just drag him into the station without a warrant," I explained, knowing he already knew that. "You heard me ask him to accompany us to the office, but he refused. Unless we get some evidence tying him to the murder, our hands are tied."

"But he's got some questions to answer!"

"We pressed him pretty hard," I explained. "I was surprised he told us as much as he did without asking for a lawyer."

Justin paced back and forth in front of Stephen's house. It looked like he was going to go charging into the house at any moment. "We've got to get this case solved," he finally said. "My supervisor called three times while y'all were inside, wanting to know how close we are to catching the killer."

"What'd you tell him?"

"The truth—we ain't got nothing yet."

I thanked Susan and began walking toward my vehicle. Justin followed my lead, and we headed to the police department.

"What are we supposed to do next?" he asked when we walked up the stairs and made our way to my office.

I tossed my keys on the desk, dropped to my chair. "I'm not real sure. We've talked to every possible witness we could talk to, interviewed every potential suspect we had, and sent every piece of evidence to the crime lab."

"Should we talk to this Zack Pitre character—?"

We both stopped and looked up as Susan stomped through the door and dropped a letter on my desk. "I don't know why I keep getting your mail in my box."

I shrugged and turned back to Justin. "Melvin and Baylor interviewed him already. Melvin said Pitre's mom claims he was home with her at the time of the murder."

Susan stopped in the doorway, indicated toward me with her left hand. "Speaking of Melvin, have you talked to him today?"

I shook my head. "Doesn't he come on tonight?"

"Yeah, he does." She scrunched her chin and I asked her what was going on. She glanced at Justin. "Can I have a word alone with Clint?"

Justin nodded and walked to the hallway. "I guess I'll call my boss and tell him we've still got nothing," he called over his shoulder. "I bet he tells me to pack it up and head home."

When Justin was out of earshot, Susan leaned closer to me. "I spoke with Melvin earlier today to tell him he could have a few days off if he needed it, but he told me he was perfectly fine."

"He wasn't fine yesterday."

"Right, but he sounded different today. He actually sounded okay, much better than he did yesterday."

I scowled. "That's a rapid turn-around."

"That's why I'm worried. Do you think he's on something? Maybe..." she hesitated and I knew where this was going.

"Are you wondering if he's drinking or self-medicating?"

She nodded.

"I can talk to him and find out."

"Thanks. I appreciate it." She pushed off of my desk and hooked a thumb over her gun belt. "I'm just worried about him."

"So am I." She walked to her office and I walked to the lobby, where Justin was arguing with his supervisor on the phone.

"Just give me one more day," he was saying. "I know we're close."

I stood waiting for him to finish the conversation. When he finally said good-bye, he sucked in some air and exhaled forcibly. "We've got twenty-four hours to solve this thing or they're pulling me back to Baton Rouge. He said we've got two other fatal fires in the western part of the state that need my attention."

"I guess we'd better get to it then." I pushed my way outside, where the temperature had cooled to about seventy-eight degrees. "But I have to check in on Melvin first."

When I arrived at Melvin's house, I asked Justin to give me a few minutes, and I got the feeling he was growing tired of being left out of our inter-departmental business. I had to knock several times before Melvin opened the door. A towel hung around his shoulders and water dripped from his ears.

"Hey, Clint, I just finished taking a shower." He craned his neck to see past me. "Is that Justin? What's going on? Did y'all catch the person who tried to shoot me?"

"No, and I'm sorry we haven't yet."

He shrugged. "I know how it goes. You'll get him before long. So, what's up?"

"I was worried about you—wondering if you're okay to go back to work."

He grinned, and it appeared genuine. "I'm perfectly fine, thanks to the meeting last night." He quickly lifted a hand. "Don't get me wrong, I still have my moments of doubt and I smell Lance's burnt flesh often. But I learned something last night that's helping me cope with what happened."

I was having my doubts that one meeting could have such a profound impact on someone. "Oh, yeah, what'd you learn? It might be helpful to me someday."

"I just imagined that Lance did something so horrible in his past life that he deserved to be burned alive."

I nodded slowly, studying Melvin's face. He wasn't joking. "And it worked?"

"It did."

"What on earth did you imagine?"

He shook his head. "You don't want to know."

I must've been staring at him with a weird expression on my face, because he asked what was wrong.

"Nothing at all. You just gave me an idea." We made small talk for a minute and I told him to call if he needed anything.

I sauntered back to my Tahoe, where Justin was talking on his cell phone to another fire marshal. He was giving him instructions on processing a fire scene. When he ended the call, he shook his head. "We've got two new agents and they're catching some complicated fires. I'm having a hard time convincing my supervisor to let me stay down here for the twenty-four hours he promised."

"Well, Melvin offered a new perspective on this whole case."

"And what's that?"

"What if Lance did something so awful in his past life that he deserved to be burned alive?"

Justin rubbed his chin in thought. "I can only think of a few sins worthy of that kind of punishment, but if he did commit those sins, this would be a justifiable homicide, indeed."

"I used to say if we find the motive, then we find the killer. If we can find out what sin Lance committed, we should be able to narrow down the pool of suspects."

"Don't you mean broaden the pool of suspects? As it stands now, we've narrowed it done to nothing."

I recognized that he did have a point, parked under the police department building and shut off my engine. We walked down the street for some burgers. After they were ready, we brought them back to my office and ate while we began scouring through police records, Internet search engines, and digital news reports, trying to find every incident in which his name was mentioned.

"Any luck?" I asked after about an hour of searching.

"There were some people saying some things about him on his Facebook page, but nothing worth killing over. One man was angry because Lance closed a deal on a house for him and the man found out he had termites a year later. He wrote, *If Lance will lie about termites, what won't he lie about?* And he misspelled termites." Justin shrugged. "It's a weak motive, though. It's not like Lance planted the termites."

"How do you know?" I countered. "Let's say he *did* plant the termites—would the man be justified in burning him alive?"

"Not only would he be justified, but it would be symbolic. Fire is about the only thing that can kill a termite."

"What's the man's name?"

He told me and I wrote it down. I ran a name inquiry and found out the man had two priors, one for DWI. "Well, that's a start. Anyone else?"

Justin shook his head. "Nope, that's it. Seems no one had a real beef with him."

"Let's try his wife." I packed up my notes and shoved them into a file, and we set out to find Mrs. Beaman. It wasn't hard. She was sitting on her front porch reading a Bible. I waved as we approached. "How are you feeling, Mrs. Beaman?"

"Someone murdered my husband...how the hell do you think I feel?"

"I'm sorry, ma'am. Poor choice of words."

She sighed, waved her forgiveness. "Please, come on inside. I've got some fresh lemonade."

I was surprised how friendly she was being, considering the way she'd spoken to me the last time. I scanned the area for news vans, just in case they were lying in wait.

"Does everyone in this town make lemonade?" Justin asked out of the corner of his mouth as we followed her across the porch. He tried to speak low enough so only I would hear, but he failed miserably.

"They might make lemonade," Mrs. Beaman said, "but they don't make it fresh. I pick my own lemons off my own tree and squeeze them myself."

He flashed a sheepish grin, asked for a glass. "If you go through all that trouble, the least I can do is drink it."

Once we were seated around her table, she slid an announcement card in my direction. "These are the details on the service. I would like y'all to be there."

"Wouldn't miss it," I said. "Again, I'm truly sorry for your loss."

"So am I, young man, so am I." She dabbed at her right eye with a dish towel and set about pouring three glasses of yellow refreshment. She placed a glass in front of both of us and then sat down with her own. "What can I do for you gentlemen?"

"We're trying to delve into Lance's past and see if there's anyone who might have a beef against him, someone who might want to harm him."

"There's only one person who wished him ill, and that was Pauline Cain. I already told you it was her, so why hasn't she been arrested yet? I told that reporter the same thing I told you—about the affair and everything—and they were eager to hear about it."

I scowled. "I wish you hadn't done that."

"Why? So you can protect your precious little boss?"

"No, ma'am…so I can control what information gets out to the public. The killer is still out there, so the less the general public knows while the case is ongoing, the better for us."

"The way I figure," she countered, "the more people who know, the better the chances of Pauline cracking and 'fessing up. That woman will fold under pressure, I just know it."

Justin and I took turns asking Mrs. Beaman more questions about Lance, but she would not say a bad thing about the man. According to her, everyone loved him and he'd never had so much as an argument with anyone other than Pauline.

I left there wondering if I was wrong about Pauline. What if her alibi witness was in on the murder and they were covering for each other? Stranger things had happened in criminal cases. And if so, how would I prove it?

CHAPTER 31

Monday, May 1

It had been eight days since Lance Beaman was burned to death, and I was still no closer to solving his case than I was in the first minutes of the investigation. "How's my tie?" I asked Susan, who was standing beside me in our bathroom.

She grabbed my shoulder and twisted my body until I was facing her, smirked when she saw the knot in my tie. "You still doing that half-Windsor thing?"

"That what?"

"The knot—it's a half-Windsor."

"Oh, I call it the slanted knot." When she had finished jerking it here and pushing it there, I turned toward the mirror. I looked tired, but that was to be expected. True to his word, Justin's supervisor had called him back to Baton Rouge exactly twenty-four hours after promising to give him twenty-four hours, and I'd been left to work the case alone. I didn't mind, though, because I enjoyed working alone. What I didn't like was hitting dead ends.

I'd spent most of the week canvassing the Mechant Loup-North neighborhood—I did it three times—but didn't turn up anything. I even spread out into the surrounding neighborhoods, hitting North Pine especially hard, but met with the same results.

I collected the names and dates of birth of every resident in the area—none of whom refused to provide the information—and their recent visitors. I ran every name up, down, and sideways through every database available to law enforcement, but didn't turn up any red flags.

I interviewed the man who had left the comment on Lance's Facebook page, but his alibi was solid. In my canvass of the neighborhoods, I'd viewed the footage of every home surveillance system I could find. Still, I didn't turn up a single shred of evidence that would help me identify who had killed Lance and taken shots at Melvin.

"Want me to go to the funeral with you?" Susan pulled on her uniform shirt and zipped it up, then fastened the buttons in place. "I can attend as the chief of police, but I can be an extra set of eyes."

I nodded and thanked her. Even if Mrs. Beaman hadn't invited me, I was going to attend anyway. Someone wanted Lance dead and I'd investigated everyone with an obvious motive, but I kept coming up empty. And the more I came up empty, the more I started thinking I was wrong about Pauline. Hell, I was even starting to dream up ways to covertly obtain fingerprints and a DNA sample from her.

I had received a call from the lab two days ago to let me know they'd developed a DNA profile from the flint wheel of the lighter. They had run it through the Combined DNA Index System (CODIS) but there hadn't been a hit.

That, along with the fact that the fingerprints from the lighter were not in AFIS and there was no match on the shell casings in IBIS, led me to believe this killing was not perpetrated by a documented criminal. If this person was a criminal, he or she had never been caught yet. If this person wasn't a criminal, it could be anyone—and that included Pauline Cain.

"Ready or not," I said, "it's time to go."

Susan never wore much makeup, and she didn't need to. I thought it was a sin for a woman that beautiful to cover up God's handiwork with something man had created. She didn't make an exception for the funeral. After putting on a little lipstick, she followed me outside and we headed for the church in separate vehicles. She pulled off the road about a mile from the church and let me drive up first so it wouldn't be obvious that we were there together.

I scowled when I saw two news vans in the church parking lot. A cameraman was filming a news reporter who was saying something while pointing toward the church. No doubt she was saying that the body of Lance Beaman was inside of *that* building and his case remained unsolved. I knew they would bombard me with questions, so I drove around to the back and slipped in the rear entrance.

"Detective Wolf," Chet said when he recognized me, "I'm so glad you could make it."

"I wouldn't miss it, sir." I shook his hand, fielded a dozen questions about the status of the case. When he had exhausted his inquiry, I made my way past him and toward the front of the church, where Mrs. Beaman was standing with her son and four or five other people I didn't recognize.

I wasn't Catholic, but I stopped near the casket to pay my respects to the remains of her husband. The casket was closed, as would be expected, and I wondered if Mrs. Beaman had been allowed to view her husband's body.

"Did you find my husband's killer?" Mrs. Beaman asked loudly when I turned from the casket to shake her hand. Her eyes seemed to focus on a spot somewhere deep in my forehead. I knew she must've been taking something to help her cope with her loss, but it seemed she was not taking it as prescribed, because the changes in her mood over the past few times I'd seen her were noticeable.

I frowned. "I'm sorry, ma'am, but I'm working the case night and day, and I won't rest until justice is served."

She grunted and turned away from me. Not wanting to upset her more, I simply walked off and stood to the left side of the church where I could monitor the folks who walked up to greet her. If I couldn't find the killer outside of the family, I would have to look to Lance's inner circle. He had a son, two daughters, and six grandchildren, but only one of the grandchildren was old enough to formulate the intent to commit murder. I studied his children as they maneuvered through the crowd, greeting people, laughing, crying—probably sharing fond memories of their father.

I even eyed Mrs. Beaman for a long moment. What if she wanted her husband dead? Of course, it wasn't as simple as wanting the man dead. If that's what she wanted, she could've just put a bullet in him. No, I had to ask myself what would make a wife so angry that she'd want to burn her husband alive. Minor infractions such as leaving his beard shavings in the sink, forgetting the toilet seat up, or snoring too loudly might piss off a wife, but not to this level. No, this was serious.

Infidelity, perhaps? It was one of the oldest motives for murder. As soon as the thought entered my mind, I started to dismiss it. I couldn't wrap my mind around a woman burning her husband alive for adultery, but then I paused to consider the emotions that were involved in an adulterous relationship. I actually knew a few women who often argued vehemently that adultery should be a criminal offense and the punishment should be death, so this was definitely not out of the realm of possibilities.

But, if Lance had been unfaithful to his wife, with whom had he cheated?

I scanned the women in the room, trying to find someone who appeared out of place and who was more emotional than the other guests. I didn't find anyone fitting that description. I did see Susan at the back of the church speaking to the funeral home director. I smiled when she looked in my direction. She smiled back and began to work the crowd.

I was beginning to think I'd hit a dead end when I noticed a man at the back of the line of people who were waiting to pay their respects. The line had dwindled, but there were still a half dozen people in front of him. He was an older gentleman, probably in his mid-sixties, and he was dressed nice enough. A gray suit coat with matching slacks, a white shirt that had been starched to perfection, and shiny black shoes. He had a head of thick hair and a neatly trimmed beard that matched his wardrobe. It wasn't his clothes or his grooming habits that caught my attention. It was his forehead and his eyes.

There were droplets of sweat forming at his hairline and his eyes shifted nervously about as he moved closer to the casket. No one seemed to be paying him much attention, so I figured he was either a family member or a personal friend. When there was only one slender lady left in line ahead of him, he licked his lips and took a deep breath. I leaned forward, wondering what he was going to do.

I wanted to glance over at Mrs. Beaman to see if she noticed the man, but I didn't want to miss what was about to happen. The slender lady finally turned from the casket and made her way to Mrs. Beaman. The man in gray stepped fully in front of the casket, made the sign of the cross, and—

What the hell?

CHAPTER 32

No one seemed to notice the man in gray as he hurried past Lance's family and headed in my direction. Our eyes locked for a brief moment as he brushed by me, heading for the main entrance to the church. I scanned the service hall for Susan and saw her speaking with a group of people dressed in black. I couldn't get her attention, so I spun from my spot and began following the man. I needed to know more about him, so I couldn't let him get away. He very well could be the person who killed Lance and attempted to murder Melvin.

The man had increased his step and was walking with his head down. I matched his pace, still trying to catch Susan's eye.

I was ten steps away when the man slipped through the large painted glass doors. Pausing by the door so he wouldn't think I was following him, I glanced back at Susan one last time. She was staring right at me with a quizzical expression on her face. I shot my right hand to my face—thumb to my ear and pinky to my mouth—to signal for her to call me, and then pushed through the door.

Careful to act nonchalant, I strode down the steps with my head down, but my eyes were studying the church parking lot. It wasn't hard to find the man. He was walking briskly toward my left, digging for his keys as he hurried along. I was parked in the back, but I needed to see what kind of car he drove and what direction he—

"Detective Wolf," called an excited voice. "Are you any closer to solving the Lance Beaman murder case?"

"No comment." I turned left to make my way around the back of the church. I could feel the presence of the news reporter behind me. The man in gray had stopped near a light blue car and was quickly getting inside. I turned on my heel to face the reporter. "Is there a reason you're following me?"

The woman pulled up short. "I just wanted to ask you a few questions."

"I'm not going to answer them. Is there anything else?"

She hesitated, then shook her head.

"Great, if there's anything else I can help you with, just go ahead and contact the office." I whirled around and made the corner of the church, but not before I saw that the man was heading north on the highway in his blue car. There was a red bumper sticker on the right side of his back bumper, so I knew it would be easy to identify his car.

My phone rang just as I reached my vehicle and fired it up. Without looking, I knew it was Susan. "I think I've got something," I said as I reached the highway and turned north, trying not to squeal my tires and alert the reporter that I was on to something. "I'm heading north on Main following a blue car with a red bumper sticker."

"Who's in the car?"

"I don't know—a man who spat on Lance's coffin. I need you to secure that casket and collect the man's DNA."

There was a pause on the other end and I could almost feel Susan turning to look toward the casket. "A man spat on Lance's coffin in front of his family?"

"Yeah, but no one seemed to notice." I tapped my brakes as the blue car slowed for a red light up ahead. I glanced at the space on the rear bumper where the license plate should be. There was a hand-written sign stating the license had been applied for. That was illegal and it was enough to justify a traffic stop, but I didn't want to blow my cover. I didn't care about a traffic violation—I needed to know if this man was a killer. "Can you recover the DNA and have it sent to the lab? If it matches the DNA from the lighter, we've got our man."

"Sure, but it could be days before we get the results back—even if they put a rush on it."

"I know."

"What are you going to do in the meantime?"

I shoved on my sunglasses so the man wouldn't see me studying his face in his rearview mirror. "I'm going to find out who this man is and why he hates Lance."

"Okay—just be careful."

CHAPTER 33

Once I'd swiped my thumb across the screen to end the call with Susan, I tossed my phone into the cup holder. The man had driven forward when the traffic light turned green. He glanced into his mirrors occasionally as we ventured into Central Chateau, but he didn't seem bothered by the fact that I was behind him. He was traveling a few miles under the speed limit, so a line of cars had gathered behind us.

On the rural roads of our parish, many folks considered the speed limit signs suggestions rather than rules, and most of them ignored the "suggestion" to drive fifty-five miles per hour. Now, two bikers decided to pass us up in a no-passing zone. They zipped past me and were overtaking the blue car when I saw the driver window slide down. The man shoved his hand out of the window and flipped off the bikers while laying on the horn.

I scowled. *Why are you so pissed off about being passed up when you're driving under the speed limit?*

The bikers returned the one-finger salute and sped off, their engines roaring like lions. The man continued cruising along until he came to Lincoln Highway, where he headed west toward St. Claiborne, which was an outlying town in Chateau Parish. We traveled for about twenty minutes before his left blinker flashed brightly. He turned onto a two-lane road and I kept going straight through the intersection, watching him with one eye as I kept the other on the road.

When he was out of sight, I made a U-turn in the middle of the road and sped back to the intersection. Two cars had turned in behind him, and they provided cover for me. I remained about a quarter of a mile behind the last car and followed for about two miles, at which time the man in the blue car made another left onto a narrow shell street that was lined on either side by trailers and mobile homes.

A faded wooden sign at the entrance to the street announced that he was entering Beasley Trailer Park. Another sign warned that visitors should drive five miles per hour to keep the dust down, or risk being banned from the property.

I pulled to the shoulder to give him space. When I thought he'd gone far enough, I turned in and made my way at a crawling pace. The shell road snaked along, making sharp turns to the left and right as it zigzagged toward the end of the trailer park. I had almost reached the end of the street—it felt like it had taken an hour—when I spotted the blue car in front of a brown and tan trailer.

The man had parked near a large green garbage can with the number "626" painted on the side of it. He was just shutting off his car, so I quickly pulled into a bumpy driveway about a block away and on the opposite side of the street.

"Can I help you?" asked an elderly lady wearing a garden apron and holding a basket of what appeared to be fresh-laid eggs. I had been so busy watching the man exit his car and disappear from my sight around the trailer that I hadn't noticed the woman working in her yard.

Thinking quickly, I leaned out of my window. "I'm sorry, ma'am, but I'm looking for a friend of mine. Is this Beasley Trailer Park?"

"It is." The woman switched her basket from one hand to the other. There were a lot of eggs in it, and I imagined it must've been heavy. "Who's your friend?"

I turned back toward the blue car. The man hadn't reappeared. I shoved my thumb toward the trailer. "You know what? I think that's it over there."

The woman scowled. "Are you sure about that?"

"I'm pretty sure."

"Well, I'm pretty sure it ain't." She stepped closer and glanced into my Tahoe. "Are you an officer?"

"I am. I'm working undercover and I'm not doing a very good job of it, am I?"

She grunted. "So, this bit about your friend, is that your cover story?"

I sighed, shot my thumb in the direction of the blue car once again. "I need to know the name of the man who lives in that trailer."

"The name's Delvin Miller. I knew he wasn't your friend,

because he doesn't have any friends. The man's a recluse. He's never had a visitor as long as I've been living here." She indicated with her head toward a neighboring trailer. "Mona's been here longer than me, and she says she's never seen a visitor either. He's got no family, no friends, no nothing. He comes and goes from time to time, but most days he just stays home."

"And he lives alone?" I asked.

She nodded.

An idea suddenly occurred to me. "Do you mind if I park my unit here?"

"For how long?"

"A few minutes."

The woman shrugged. "I guess so. As long as I can get out later. I need to make a grocery bill."

"I won't be long." I thanked her and dropped from my Tahoe, headed across the street. Delvin's trailer was positioned perpendicular to the shell street, and all I could see was the back and front end of his residence. I kept a wary eye on the windows and back door as I approached. When I reached the opposite shoulder, I fell into an idle stroll, trying to appear as a random fellow out enjoying the afternoon sun.

More of the front yard came into view as I drew closer to the trailer. For the most part, it was well groomed and free of litter, something I couldn't say about many of the other trailers in the area. It became obvious by the hand-painted signs that Mr. Miller didn't appreciate trespassers and he owned a gun—or, at least, he wanted violators to think he owned a gun.

I had finally reached the garbage can and was about to push the lid open when it caught my eye. The sun was high in the sky and I squinted to try and make out what I was seeing. Still not sure, I put a hand to my forehead and stepped forward, straining to make out the two objects that were positioned side-by-side and toward the rear of his property. I sucked in a mouthful of air when I realized what they were.

At the center of the yard there was a large, round bed of loose rocks that were held in place by a circle of larger rocks. Buried at the center of this bed of rocks, and facing the front door of the trailer, were twin crosses that stood at least four feet tall. They were made of solid wood and painted red. They each bore a name, but they were too far away for me to make out the names.

I scanned the front of the trailer, cocking my head to the side to listen for any sound of movement from inside. There was none.

Crouching low so as not to be seen from the nearest window, I slid along the trailer, taking one step at a time and then stopping, listening to see if my actions had brought a response from inside. When it hadn't, I moved another step closer to the center of the trailer. After a few long minutes, I was directly across from the crosses and could read what was painted on them.

The one on the left read:

Lacie Marie Miller
Born: September 21, 1979
Murdered: June 16, 1997

The one on the right read:

Macie Marie Miller
Born: September 21, 1979
Murdered: June 16, 1997

I immediately pulled out my phone, took several pictures. My mind raced. If these crosses bore the truth, Delvin Miller's twin daughters had been murdered twenty years ago, at the age of seventeen. I hadn't been in this parish for many years, so I wouldn't have been around when the murders occurred, but I wondered why I hadn't at least heard whisperings about it. Just the news that a pair of twins had died on the same day would live on for many years, but being murdered together? That's the kind of thing that could turn into folklore.

Once I had the pictures I needed, I scurried along the trailer, making my way back to the garbage can. I reached it just as I heard some footsteps pounding inside the trailer. It sounded as though they were heading for the front door.

Working quickly—my pulse racing—I lifted the lid on the garbage can and peered inside. There were two plastic bags, and both were filled with garbage. I grabbed the bag that seemed to have the most garbage, lowered the lid carefully, and then headed up the street. I heard a door slam from somewhere behind me and quickened my pace. While I wasn't worried about a confrontation, I certainly didn't want my cover being blown. If Delvin was our killer, it was best if he didn't know we were on to him.

I glanced over my shoulder just as I reached my Tahoe. All was clear. I opened the back gate and tossed the bag inside. The woman in the garden apron was sitting on her porch.

"Did you get what you needed?" she asked.

I nodded, asked if I could camp out in her yard for a while.

"Just as long as you move when I need to go to the store and then when I get back."

CHAPTER 34

"Susan, can you meet me at Beasley Trailer Park in an unmarked car?" I asked, giving her the address.

"Isn't that in St. Claiborne?"

"It is." I explained what I'd found in Delvin Miller's yard and told her about the bag I'd lifted from the garbage. "I'm keeping an eye on the trailer and can't leave until we know if this is our guy or not. I need someone to go through the trash and find his fingerprints, then have it compared to the print from the lighter."

"You need someone to do your dirty work, is that it?"

"I guess you could say that." I shifted in my seat when I saw movement in the area of Delvin's trailer, but settled into place when I saw a large gray cat stroll out from behind the trailer. "I called the sheriff's office and asked them to run everything they could find on Delvin Miller. I also called Mallory and asked her to check their records for a murder of a pair of twins dating back twenty years."

Mallory Tuttle was a detective with the Chateau Parish Sheriff's Office, and she was one of Susan's friends.

I could hear Susan react on the other end of the phone. "I've *never* heard of twins being murdered in Chateau—and I don't care how long ago it happened. It could've been fifty years and people would still be talking about that kind of thing. The fact that it supposedly happened while I was alive makes me think it didn't happen here."

My phone buzzed in my ear. I glanced at the screen. "I have to go," I said. "The sheriff's office is beeping in."

"Okay, I'll meet you there in twenty minutes."

I pressed the green dot on the screen to answer the call. "What's the good news?"

"Clint, I ran a criminal history check on the name you gave me, but turned up nothing."

"Does he have a driver's license?"

"Yeah, a Louisiana one, but he's never even had a ticket as far as I could tell—at least not here. If he got one in some small jurisdiction it wouldn't show up on my records."

I nodded thoughtfully, thanked her and hung up. While Delvin was clean, it didn't mean he didn't kill Lance. I'd worked a number of homicide cases where the murder I was investigating happened to be the first criminal act the suspect had ever committed. People killed for any number of reasons. If I was a betting man, I'd bet that Delvin's apparent hatred of Lance Beaman had something to do with those two crosses in his yard. Of course, just because he spat on the man's casket didn't mean he was the one who put him in it.

I was tempted to walk right across the street and knock on the trailer door, but I needed some sort of evidence before I made contact with him. If Susan could recover one of his prints from the contents of the garbage bag and then match it to the lighter, I'd have the leverage I needed. So, I just sat there watching and waiting.

Susan showed up about twenty minutes after we'd hung up and I gave her the garbage bag. She called me an hour later to say she'd recovered several fingerprints from an empty aluminum soda can, a plastic jar of peanut butter, and a glass jar of pickles. She'd concluded that the prints were from the same person. "I made a one-to-one digital image of the prints and emailed them to the lab," she'd said. "They're supposed to get back to me within the hour."

That was almost three hours ago. The sun was starting to set to the west and lights were starting to flicker to life up and down the street. A light came on in Delvin's house, but the curtains were drawn and I couldn't see inside. The woman in whose yard I was parked came out several times to check on me. On one of her trips, she'd brought me a plate of fried pork meat atop a heaping mound of rice and a cold bottle of root beer. I must've been hungry because that was the best pork I'd ever eaten. I thanked her repeatedly, but she just waved her hand dismissively. "I can't have you dying of hunger on my watch," she'd said. "That would ruin my reputation."

It was completely dark when Susan finally called back. "It's not his print," she said simply.

She said it so nonchalantly that I had to blink several times before the news sank in. "Wait—he's not our killer?"

"I didn't say that. I just said it's not his print."

"Are you sure?"

"Have you heard from Mallory?" She'd deliberately ignored my question.

I sighed. "Not yet."

"If I know her, she's still searching. She won't stop until she finds something, and she'll call you as soon as she does." Before hanging up, she told me she was heading home. "I have to check on one of our residents at the shelter. Her husband bonded out today and I need to make sure she doesn't make contact with him and give away the location."

I sat staring at Delvin's trailer for a long moment. While I didn't have a shred of evidence to suggest he killed Lance, I knew for a fact he'd spat on the man's casket. That had to mean something.

To hell with it! I fired up my engine and drove straight for his driveway. Before I could talk myself out of it, I dropped from the Tahoe and marched to the front steps. I banged loudly on the door. I was out of my jurisdiction, so I didn't identify myself. Instead, I stood back and waited for him to answer the door.

"Can I help you?" Delvin said when he pushed the door open. He had a cautious way about him, and he kept part of his body shielded from my view. There was no doubt in my mind he had a pistol in his left hand, which was hidden behind the door.

"I'd like to talk to you about Lance Beaman," I began slowly, studying his face as I mentioned the name. The wrinkle lines on his face disappeared as his expression hardened.

"What about?"

"I saw you at the funeral and I realized there was someone out there who hated the bastard as much as I did." I saw his face relax a little and I stepped closer to the door. "I'm not ashamed to say I rejoiced when I found out he was dead—especially when I found out how he died. If anyone deserved to burn to death, it was that evil prick."

"What do you want from me?" he asked.

"I just wanted to know what it was that he'd done to you," I explained, thinking quickly. "My therapist said I should seek out like-minded individuals with whom to discuss my feelings. She thinks it would be productive, but I believe hatred loves company."

Delvin was thoughtful, then he let the door swing open wider. I saw the pistol in his left hand and nodded toward it. "What's that for?"

"No one ever knocks on my door." He waved the barrel to invite me to follow him. "I was about to turn in for the night, but I'll give you a few minutes."

When we were seated at the table, he placed the pistol on the counter behind him and reached for a pack of cigarettes that protruded from his shirt pocket. "I saw you at the funeral," he said. "You didn't look happy to be there."

"I wasn't."

He lit the cigarette with a disposable lighter and took a long drag. He blew out the smoke and stared at me through squinty eyes. "You followed me here?"

I nodded. Without being obvious, I'd given the pistol a good once-over and knew it was a 9 mm. I wanted to ask him for permission to bring it to the lab and have it examined, but resisted the urge. He might say yes, but he might also say no and get rid of it before I could develop enough evidence to recover it legally.

"I saw you leave the church and I was curious to know why someone would walk into a church and spit on a dead man's casket." I turned up my hands. "That takes some courage."

"It doesn't take courage to spit on the coffin of a piece of shit like Lance Beaman." His eyes flashed. "He's lucky he got to live as long as he did. My daughters didn't get that chance."

CHAPTER 35

I waited until Delvin's breathing returned to normal and the red faded from his eyes before indicating toward the front of the trailer where the crosses were located. "Lacie and Macie...they were your daughters?"

He nodded solemnly. "Twins. The most beautiful pair you could ever imagine. They were inseparable."

"Do you mind telling me what happened?"

Although Delvin lowered his eyes, I could see them moisten.

"They were seventeen, had graduated a few weeks earlier. I didn't want them going out that night, but their mom insisted on letting them spread their wings and fly." He shook his head. "They were too young to be going out at night, even if there were two of them. No dad in his right mind would've allowed it. But they were begging and their mom joined in. It was three against one, don't you see? I finally gave in and let them go." He pinched the bridge of his nose and I could tell he was fighting back the tears.

My mind raced. What on earth had Lance done to bring about their deaths? I wanted to know what had happened and I wanted to know right now, but I didn't want to rush him. After several long minutes, he slowly opened his eyes.

"It was a concert in Baton Rouge," he said. "They drove out there and met some friends who were attending LSU. I was worried sick until they called from a payphone to say they'd made it. Three and a half hours later they called from the same payphone to say they were heading back home."

I sat patiently, my hands folded in front of me on the table. The pale light from the ceiling above cast eerie shadows across his face and traced bright lines down his cheeks where the tears were sliding freely.

"It only takes about two hours to get here from Baton Rouge, and we knew they should've been home by now. The wife and I decided to set out and look for them. She went along one route and I went along the other." He shook his head slowly. "I knew it was them when I was a mile away. I could see flames in the sky and I heard sirens in the distance. When I reached the scene, their car was engulfed in flames. A police officer and several firemen were trying to get them out—"

His voice broke up, he clutched his throat.

I scowled, waiting for him to continue. It sounded like the twins had been involved in a car crash. Was Lance the driver of the other vehicle? Had he been drunk?

"They were so close to the house." Saliva and tears sprayed from his mouth as he spoke. "They had made it all that way only to have a group of drunken assholes hit them head-on. They never had a chance." He wiped his face, but it did no good. More tears just rained down and flooded his flesh again. "Their car veered off the road, slammed into a guard rail, and burst into flames. The coroner, he said they died instantly and they didn't feel a thing. I wish I could believe him."

I shifted my feet, wanting to console the man, but not knowing how. I was also curious. He had said "group" of drunken assholes, so I found myself wondering who had been with Lance. I figured if I waited long enough, he would answer my questions, but he didn't. He just bent over, plopped his head in his hands, and wept.

My phone suddenly rang and he jumped in his skin. I quickly shut it off, took the opportunity to ask a question. "So," I asked tentatively, "who were the drunken assholes?"

"Huh?" He lifted his head and I almost gasped out loud. His face was rosy red and swollen and veins protruded like spider webs across his temple. I thought he was going to have a stroke.

"Are you okay?" I asked.

"I haven't been okay since that night," he said weakly. "There were three men in the car that hit them. Lance Beaman, Carl Wainwright, and Jack Billiot—"

"Wait...Jack Billiot?" I asked, interrupting him. "Jack Billiot from Mechant Loup?"

"They were all from Mechant Loup, and they were all drunk. Carl was driving and he died on the scene, but any one of them could've been driving. In my mind, they were all guilty." He rubbed his face.

"Since then, I've spent every minute of my life wishing Lance and Jack would die, too, thinking it would somehow bring me peace. Now that they're gone, I realize it hasn't."

I nodded absently, then stopped when I realized what he'd said. "Are you saying Jack Billiot is dead?"

"I sure hope so, because I attended his funeral and spat on his coffin just like I spat on Lance's coffin."

"When was his funeral?"

"The week before Lance died. Alcohol poisoning or something is what I heard someone say at the funeral." Delvin's face twisted into an evil scowl. "I only wish he and Carl would have burned up like Lance."

I couldn't believe I hadn't heard about Jack. "How'd you find out about Jack's death?"

"The obituaries...I read them every day." Delvin looked at me like I was an alien. "Don't you read them?"

I shook my head, stared deep into his eyes. He certainly had motive to kill Lance. Hell, if he *did* kill Lance, a jury would probably find him not guilty after hearing all he'd been through.

"Can you tell me anything else about that night? The night of the crash?"

He stared absently at his hands. "I remember seeing Lance and Jack sitting together on the guard rail. I tried to run at them, but a cop stopped me."

"Did they say anything to you?"

He shook his head.

"Can you remember anything else? Anything that might help me find a report?"

He was thoughtful, then recounted the date of the crash and the location. "That's about all I know."

I was thoughtful myself, wondering why now. If he had killed Lance, why would he wait twenty years to exact revenge? What had changed in all of that time? And why would he only go after Lance? What about Jack?

"Did you ever say anything to anyone about the crash?"

"I did. I spoke to Mayor Cain when Lance first announced his candidacy for mayor. I told her he and his friends had killed my daughters and he didn't deserve to be mayor. I wanted her to expose him for what he was, but she refused to turn to dirty politics. I guess I respect her for that now, but I was angry at the time. I just wanted justice for my babies." Delvin was crying again. "If you're waiting for me to say I'm sorry for spitting on those coffins, it's not going to happen. I'm glad they're both dead. I only wish I would've had the courage to kill them myself."

I suddenly felt sick to my stomach. Pauline had also lost a child, so she knew firsthand the everlasting pain that came with such a loss. Had she been so overcome with pity for poor Delvin Miller that she made Lance pay for what he had done? She already hated Lance, and this could have been the proverbial "final straw".

CHAPTER 36

It was a little after ten o'clock when I finally left Delvin Miller's house. He had done a lot of talking, telling me how he'd blamed his wife for their daughters' deaths and it ultimately led to her committing suicide. He lost his job, had two nervous breakdowns, and ended up on disability. His religion was the only reason he was still alive. He said he was Catholic and suicide was a mortal sin, so all he could do was pray to die. He said he knelt in front of the twin crosses in his yard every morning, begging God to let that day be the one when he would finally get to see his daughters again.

"I believe God kept me alive long enough to see Jack and Lance pay for their sins," he'd said wistfully as I'd walked out of his house. "Now that they're gone, it won't be long before He takes me home to be with my girls."

I hadn't known what to say in response, so I'd only waved and crossed the street. I was on the phone with Susan before I reached my Tahoe. "Did you know Jack Billiot died?" I jerked the door open and jumped into the driver seat.

"Oh, yeah, he passed away two days after we left for our honeymoon," she said. "I saw it on the calls for service log and asked Takecia about it. She said she received a call about a medical emergency, a man having chest pain and difficulty breathing. The ambulance arrived and transported him to the hospital, where he died later that night."

I sat slumped over in my seat, pondering what I'd learned tonight. When Susan asked me what was going on, I told her everything Delvin had revealed. "It can't be a coincidence that Lance gets murdered five days after Jack dies," I said. "It has to mean something."

"And it can't be a coincidence that Pauline knew about Lance and the crash. Do you think we need to question her some more?"

I didn't know, so I said goodbye and drove away. It was then that I remembered the missed call from earlier. I pulled to the shoulder of the road and checked the call log. It was Mallory. Without thinking, I immediately hit *redial*. She answered on the first ring.

"Clint, thank God you're up. I found something. Can you meet me at the detective bureau?"

The detective bureau was along my route back to Mechant Loup, but even if it hadn't been, I still would've made the trip. "I'll be there in fifteen."

My mind went over every possible scenario as I drove to the detective bureau, but nothing made sense. I needed to know more about Jack's death, so I called Susan and asked her to print up a copy of Takecia's report for me. She told me she'd bring a copy home and put it on the table for me. "I'll probably be in bed by the time you get home," she said, "but you'd better kiss me goodnight before you go to sleep."

I promised to do so and parked beside Mallory's car in the bureau parking lot. I was certain Mallory had located the crash report detailing the deaths of Macie and Lacie. While I already knew about it, the least I could do was go over the information she found. After all, she'd stayed up half the night digging for it.

"Follow me to my cubicle," she said when she'd let me in. "I thought I'd have to call you with some bad news, but I hit pay dirt when I checked our storage archives. We keep major cases—mostly murder and rape files—back there, but I found a fatality crash investigation with Lance Beaman's name on the box. I thought it was odd that we'd keep such a file, but one of our deputies had gotten burned pretty bad trying to save the victims, so our department was heavily involved in the investigation."

"I just got through interviewing Mr. Delvin Miller. Is it the same crash?"

Mallory stopped walking and spun abruptly. "How'd you know about him?"

I told her what he'd done at the church.

"Well, my money's definitely on him. According to the file, he threatened to kill Lance Beaman and Jack Billiot the night of the crash, and he also said he was glad the driver was dead. They had to restrain him because he tried to attack Beaman and Billiot. In his mind, they were all guilty of murder."

I nodded and we continued to her cubicle, where she had broken the file apart. Reports and envelopes were scattered across her desktop. Sticky notes littered her desktop and she had marked up a copy of the report.

"Was Miller right about Carl Wainwright being the driver?" I picked up the crash report and began thumbing through it.

"Yeah, he died at the scene." Mallory handed me several worn envelopes that contained pictures from the crash. Some were labeled "CPSO" (Chateau Parish Sheriff's Office) and others were labeled "LSP" (Louisiana State Police). The first photo in the first envelope depicted a young man—bloodied and broken—slumped in the driver seat of an old sedan.

I studied the man behind the steering wheel. His features were indiscernible thanks to the mess of blood and mangled flesh. I flipped through the pictures. Most were of the driver, some overall views, a few mid-range, and lots of close-ups. I scowled as I reached a photo of his lower extremities. I stabbed it with an index finger. "Mallory, did you notice he's missing a shoe?"

Mallory turned from a lab report she was reading, studied the photo. "No, I hadn't noticed."

"How'd he lose his shoe?"

She shrugged. "He was involved in a car crash. Clothes and shoes are regularly ripped from bodies during car crashes."

She was right, of course, but I wanted to know where his shoe had ended up. I flipped through the stack in my hand, then reached for another envelope. Considering it had been a fatal crash, I wasn't surprised by the large number of photos in the envelopes.

Mallory and I made small talk as I sifted through the photographs and she studied the autopsy reports on everyone involved. I caught sight of Lance Beaman in the background of several of the pictures and was surprised by how different he looked. He was much thinner and his hair was much thicker. He looked disheveled and—even from a distance—I could see that his eyes were wide in one of the shots.

"Oh, damn, this is eerie." Mallory lifted the report detailing the injuries to the deputy who had been burned. "I remember him from my police academy. He gave a talk about the hazards of the job. He took off his shirt and showed us his back." She shuddered. "It was horrendous."

I nodded absently, still studying the photographs. "How'd he get burned?"

"Something exploded in the car—they think it was an aerosol

can." She grunted. "Considering when this crash happened, it was probably hairspray."

I nodded and studied the picture in my hand. I was about to flip it to the back of the pile when I caught sight of something red on the side of the road near the back passenger door. It was at the corner of the photograph, barely visible in the shot, but I was pretty sure I knew what it was. I checked the next photograph and there it was, plain as day—a red shoe.

I shoved the photos back in the envelope and picked up the next one, which was the first that was labeled "LSP". I thumbed quickly through them, as there were many repetitive shots, but froze when I reached a photo depicting the area near the back passenger door of the sedan. Aside from a shift in angle, it looked identical to the photo from the sheriff's office, with the huge exception of the red shoe being gone. I flipped through the other shots of the same area and it had definitely been moved. I tapped the desk, thinking. I knew it could've easily been inadvertently kicked by a first responder. Considering how chaotic and active the scene would've been, that was more likely than not.

I shrugged, thumbed through the next envelope of LSP photographs. I located more photographs of the driver's area, sucked in my breath when I caught sight of something. I then quickly flipped back through the photos, searching for one I'd seen of Lance. I stopped when I found it. He was bloodied and disheveled, but he was on his feet. I pulled the photo close to my face and studied his expression. He looked disturbed, which was to be expected, but he also looked guilty about something. I then searched until I located one of Jack Billiot, who was also injured, but his injuries didn't appear life-threatening. Having had a number of dealings with Jack in town, I was a little familiar with his mannerisms, and he looked like he was hiding something.

I shuffled back through the sheriff's office photos until I found the one depicting the red shoe, tilted it so the light from Mallory's desk would splash across it. "Mallory, here's Carl's shoe."

"Where?" Mallory twisted around and craned her neck to see where I pointed. "There's a glare—I can't see it."

I handed it to her and her eyes widened when she saw it. "What on earth is his shoe doing outside on the passenger side of the vehicle?"

"That's what I was wondering, until I found this." I handed her the photo from one of the state police envelopes showing the red shoe on the driver floorboard.

"What the hell?"

"Carl Wainwright wasn't driving," I declared. "Lance and Jack dragged him from the back seat to the driver seat, and he lost his shoe in the process. They must've noticed their mistake and, during the chaos, one of them tossed the shoe into the front seat."

"So, they framed Carl for the crash?"

I nodded. "Since he was dead, he couldn't argue the point."

Mallory studied the photographs. "But how'd the officers miss this? It's obvious the shoe was moved."

I held the envelope from the sheriff's office in one hand and the one from the state police in the other. "The sheriff's office was investigating this as an injury incident and the state police was investigating a fatal crash. Apparently, the sheriff's office never sent their stack of photos to the state police."

"Or, if they did, no one bothered to look through them." She nodded thoughtfully. "After all, the offender was dead, so there would be no trial."

I held the stack of photos loosely, allowed my hand to rest at my side. "If Lance and Jack moved Carl to the driver's seat, then that means one of them had to be driving."

"But which one?"

"I'm not sure, and I don't know how we'll find that out now—they're both dead."

"Billiot's dead?"

I explained what Susan had said about Jack. "He was one of the town drunks…" I allowed my voice to trail off, stopped with my mouth open. "Wow, it makes perfect sense now. That's probably what led to his life of drinking."

"I've met Beaman a few times and he didn't seem to be bothered by anything," Mallory said. "His life was going great."

"It could mean he wasn't the driver," I offered, "or—if he *was* driving—he's just a cold-blooded prick."

"It had to be him or Billiot."

"Billiot died of natural causes, Beaman was murdered." I plopped the pictures on Mallory's desk. "If this is the motive we've been looking for, then someone thought Lance was driving the car that night."

Mallory shook her head. "I've gone over this entire file—page by page—and everything says Wainwright was driving. Hell, even the newspaper clippings put him as the driver. Whoever killed Beaman either knew something we didn't know or they killed him for a different reason."

"It could be Miller. He might've been frustrated that Pauline wouldn't use the information he provided, so he decided to take matters into his own hands. Unless…" A thought suddenly occurred to me. "What do sinners do right before they die?"

Mallory shrugged. "Pray for God's forgiveness?"

"No, but along those lines…"

"I give up. I don't go to church."

"They confess their sins."

Her expression was blank as she stared at me. "I'm not following you."

"If Jack Billiot knew he was going to die, he might've confessed his sins to someone." I quickly jotted down a checklist of things to do first thing in the morning, and the top thing on that list was to speak with the hospital staff to see if Jack had had any visitors before he died. "If he got word to Miller that Lance was driving, he would've put a bull's eye on the Lance's back."

CHAPTER 37

Tuesday, May 2
Chateau Parish General Hospital

I sat in the hospital parking lot staring at Takecia's report as though I hoped some hidden clue would jump off the page and smack me in the face. It was a simple report, as reports go. She had responded to a medical emergency at Jack Billiot's house on the east side, and was met at the door by his mother, who led Takecia to a back bedroom where Jack was struggling for air. Ox Plater had shown up moments later with Cole Peterson and another firefighter, and they went right to work on Jack. They stabilized him and kept him alert until the medics arrived to transport him to the hospital. Takecia had resumed her duties and received a call from the hospital later letting her know Jack had died.

Before heading to the hospital and interviewing the hospital staff here, I had stopped by the fire department and spoken with Ox and Cole. Ox hadn't heard Jack utter a word the entire time they were there, but Cole did say he remembered Jack's mother kissing him after he was stabilized, and Cole thought Jack whispered something in her ear.

"I couldn't make out what he said," Cole had recounted, "but I do know he said something."

Ox had shaken his head. "I didn't hear a damn thing, but, of course, I've got this bum ear."

I had then come to the hospital and interviewed two nurses and a doctor, but they said Jack hadn't had any visitors from the moment he came in until the time that he died. Now, I needed to check with

Jack's mother. If I was right and Jack had revealed the truth about who was driving the truck twenty years ago, that information could've gotten into the wrong hands and led to Lance's murder. A short list of suspects was dancing around in my head, and that list began with Delvin Miller. Other possibilities were siblings, aunts or uncles, and grandparents.

I did wonder if either of the girls had boyfriends from back then who might still be traumatized by the loss, and I made a mental note to look into that angle. Twenty years was a long time for a boyfriend to be hanging on to the past, but I knew how hard it had been for me to deal with the loss of Michele, so I wasn't going to overlook anything. It was one thing to break up with someone after a relationship had turned sour, but to lose that person in the middle of a flourishing relationship—it was like freezing time in its tracks. Although things had gotten easier over time, I still had my moments of guilt about moving on with Susan, so it was a constant battle for me.

I drove straight to Delvin's house after leaving the hospital, knocked on his door.

"You again?" He scowled but stepped back and let me enter his trailer. "What do you want now?"

I glanced down at his hands and then visually examined his waistline. He didn't appear to be armed.

"As a father of two victims," I began, taking a seat across from him at the table, "I thought you had the right to know about an update to the case."

He raised his eyebrows. "An update? What are you talking about? Their case has been closed for twenty years."

"Well, there's been a new development." I took a breath and studied his face. "Carl Wainwright wasn't driving that night—he wasn't the one who killed your daughters."

Delvin's face grew so pale I could almost see through him. "What do you mean? How could you possibly know that?"

I pulled out my cell phone and accessed my images, flipped to the one I'd taken of the red shoe. "This is Carl's shoe. It was on the ground outside the back passenger door, but then it disappeared in this picture"—I scrolled to the next photo—"and then reappeared in this one."

When he saw the photo of the shoe on the driver floorboard, he gasped out loud. "Someone set him up?"

"That's what it looks like."

His voice was weak. "But…if he wasn't driving, then who was?"

"It was either Lance or Jack." I continued studying his face as I allowed him to process that information. He looked genuinely shocked. "You had no idea, did you?"

He shook his head. "I've lived all this time blaming Carl Wainwright for their murders. Don't get me wrong, I blamed Lance and Jack for being with him, but Carl was the driver and he was the one I hated most. Now I...I don't know who to hate."

"Look, I need your help. I believe Jack made contact with someone and told them Lance was driving the car that night, and I believe they murdered him over it."

Delvin nodded idly. "Okay...what do you need from me?"

"I need to know who else might still be hurting over the twins' deaths. Are there any other members of your family who still grieve over them? Any friends from high school? Ex-boyfriends, perhaps?"

"No, there's no one else but me. The rest of the family and their friends have all moved on with their lives. My beautiful girls have been forgotten." He frowned and his eyes misted over. "As for me, I've truly been given a life sentence. I'll hurt until the day I die. Actually, every day gets even harder than the last. My chest gets so tied in knots sometimes that I think I'm having a heart attack. And it pleases me, because I hope for it, but...but I've never been so lucky."

Only you, right? I thought, watching Delvin fall apart on his side of the table. *No one cares about the girls anymore except for you.*

I sighed, leaned back in my chair, and allowed my eyes to drift out the open door to the crosses. I needed to eliminate Delvin as a suspect once and for all, but I'd need his cooperation to do so. I already knew his fingerprints weren't on the lighter, but that didn't necessarily mean he wasn't the killer. There was a slim chance the lighter wasn't connected to the murder at all.

"Mr. Miller," I said when he stopped crying for a while, "do you mind if I borrow your pistol for comparison purposes?"

He wiped his eyes. "Compare it to what?"

"Someone took shots at one of our officers last Tuesday. I'd like to make sure it wasn't you."

"It wasn't." Delvin stood. "Thank you for stopping by, Detective. I appreciate the update."

I hesitated, but Delvin wasn't backing down. He was done with the conversation and he wanted me gone. I nodded and stood to leave.

"If you killed Lance," I said, "I'd understand. A jury would understand. It wouldn't be right, but everyone would certainly understand."

"Thank you for stopping by, Detective."

I walked out and dug my cell phone from my pocket, called Susan. "It might be Delvin Miller, but I can't be sure."

"How'd he take the news?"

"I really believe he was surprised to find out, but I don't know who else would have the motive to kill Lance."

"Maybe we're missing something," Susan suggested. "Maybe it has nothing to do with the twins."

"Nothing to do with the election, nothing to do with the crash—nothing to do with anything." I fired up my Tahoe and backed out of the driveway. "I'm running out of places to look, Sue."

She was silent on the other end, then finally asked where I was heading.

"I'm going to pay Jack Billiot's mom a visit. See if he didn't reveal anything to her before he died."

"Well, I have to work late tonight. I'm covering for Melvin."

That immediately got my attention. "Melvin? Why—what's wrong? Is he okay?"

"Oh, yeah, everything's fine. That support group he joined is having another emergency meeting tonight at the Mechant Loup Fire Station and he wants to attend. He said it helped him the last time."

"What's the emergency?"

"Cole Peterson is struggling."

"That's good that he wants help." I remembered how the kid looked on the night of the fire, and he didn't look so great when I spoke with him earlier.

After telling Susan I'd probably be late, too, I ended the call and headed south, wondering if Jack's mom would be a dead end. So far, this was shaping up to be a cold case, and the one thing that scared me more than anything else was having an unsolved murder on my hands. If I couldn't solve this case, it would mean I'd failed the victim and his family—and that wasn't acceptable, even if Lance was a horrible person.

CHAPTER 38

It was a little past eleven when I pulled into Jack Billiot's driveway. I shut off the engine, glanced at the house. It was a narrow structure wrapped in brick that was painted green. An aluminum awning extended the entire width of the house, with the left corner hanging precariously. Three steps that were about two feet wide led up to a screen door that appeared flimsy and old. The grass was long. An old ice chest was on the side of the house and I imagined it used to hold Jack's beer.

Wondering if Jack's mom was still living there, I jumped out and strode to the steps. Since her old van wasn't in the dirt driveway, my expectations were low. The screen door was locked, so I banged on the framework. Nothing moved inside. I banged several more times, but no one came to the door. I walked around to the back door, did the same, and met with the same results.

After talking to some of the neighbors and learning that the van had left an hour earlier, I drove to the office to comb through the case file. I had a pizza delivered and worked through lunch, going over every report that had been generated and analyzing every piece of evidence we'd recovered. I called the lab and found out that the DNA from Delvin's saliva didn't match the DNA from the lighter. I asked the lab technician to send me photos of the lighter after it had been cleaned up, and they appeared in my inbox twenty minutes later. I printed them out and scattered them across my desk. While there were no initials or other obvious identifiers on the lighter, it did appear unique—

I suddenly twisted in my seat and snatched up my desk phone, dialed the number to the *Mechant Voice*, which was our local newspaper. "Ali Bridges," I said when a man answered the phone. I glanced at the time on my computer screen. "I need to speak with Ali right away."

I was put on hold for a brief moment, then Ali came on the phone. I'd first met Ali when she served as an intern for my former girlfriend, Chloe Rushing, and she now worked as a top reporter for the *Mechant Voice*.

"Ali, this is Clint," I began. "If I send you a picture, can you get it to print before today's paper goes out?"

I could almost feel her checking the clock. "Can you get it to me in five minutes?"

My fingers raced across the keyboard and I was hitting the *send* button within thirty seconds flat. "It's on the way to your inbox now."

"I'm guessing this is about the murder?"

I told her it was and expressed how important it was to identify the lighter. "Someone, somewhere, has to recognize that lighter. I need them to call me immediately if they know who it belongs to. They can remain anonymous if they want to, but I've got to know who owns it."

I heard a *ding* on her end of the call. "Got it! It'll hit the newsstands this afternoon."

I thanked her and turned back to the file on my desk. I couldn't help but remember that Delvin Miller was a smoker and he had been using a disposable lighter when I interviewed him. Could the lighter we recovered be his? But even if it was, who would know about it? The man didn't associate with many people, so if he *was* the killer, there was a chance we wouldn't be getting any tips at all.

After poring over the file for another two hours, I moved to Susan's office and shared what was left of the pizza with her, then headed outside. I walked down the street to buy a copy of the *Mechant Voice* before returning to my Tahoe. I smiled my appreciation when I saw the lighter splashed across the entire top half of the front page. I'd given Ali my cell phone number as a contact and she'd printed it in bold at the end of the article. I checked my phone now, made sure the ringer was turned up.

I then drove to Jack's house and nodded when I saw the old van in the driveway. It was almost six o'clock and I wondered what Mrs. Billiot was doing inside. On a regular day, she might've been cooking dinner for her and Jack, but I imagined her evenings of late were lonely.

I only knocked once on the screen door before the main door

slowly opened. Jack's mother peered from the slight opening and asked what I wanted. I'd only seen the woman a couple of times and didn't think she knew who I was.

"It's Clint Wolf, ma'am...with the Mechant Loup Police Department. I need to speak with you about Jack."

"My Jack's dead and y'all are still harassing him! Why don't you just leave him alone?"

"No, ma'am, I'm not here to harass anyone. I just need to find out if he said anything to you in his final moments. If he had any last words."

She didn't step from behind the door, but I could see her frowning deeply. When she didn't answer, I asked the question again, then added, "I know there was something he said in his final moments, and I need to know who might've heard him."

"Who told you that?" It was more of an accusation than a question, and I knew I had struck a nerve.

"It was about what happened twenty years ago, wasn't it?" I pressed. "He shared his secret, didn't he?"

"You need to leave here...now!" She spat the words and was about to slam the door shut when I hollered for her to wait. My voice had changed so suddenly that it shocked her into inaction. "Excuse me?"

"Look, ma'am," I said softly, "I know Jack has been troubled ever since that car accident. It ruined his life...I know it did, and so do you. It wasn't his fault that he drank every day. It was the only thing he could do to cope with what happened. I just need to find out—"

"What do you know about the accident? Did he talk to you?" She allowed the door to swing wider. "Did you see him before he passed? Did he say something to you?"

I frowned. "No, ma'am, I wasn't around when he passed, but I knew him...and he was a good man. He was troubled, that's for sure, but he was good at heart."

"He was." She dabbed at her eyes with a corner of her shirt, said, "*It was Lance,* he said to me. *It was Lance who was driving the car that killed those girls.* I asked him what he was talking about, but that was all he said. He just went quiet after that and I thought we'd lost him."

"Ma'am—and this is really important—did you tell anyone what he said? Anyone at all?"

She shook her head. "Who would I tell?"

I chewed on my lower lip, thoughtful. A growing uneasiness was starting to form in the pit of my stomach. I wasn't sure I wanted to know the answer to the next question, but I asked it anyway. "Did anyone overhear what Jack said to you?"

Jack's mother lifted a hand to her throat. "Um, I don't know for sure, but I think so."

"Who?"

"Let me see...an officer got here first and then two or three people with the fire department showed up before the ambulance did."

My heart thumping in my chest, I asked again who heard what Jack had said about Lance.

"I...I'm not sure. They were in and out. The officer got here first and then the firemen and then the ambulance people. I wasn't really paying attention to them. It...I was just so upset about Jack, you understand? I didn't really keep track of who was there when he was talking."

"I understand," I said idly, thoughtful. An idea suddenly occurred to me and it made the feeling in my stomach even worse. Hoping I was wrong, I turned and headed to my Tahoe, snatching my phone from my pocket as I did so. While firing up the engine, I called Mallory. She answered right away.

"This is Mal—"

"What's the name of the deputy who got burned trying to rescue the twins?" I asked, interrupting her introduction. "You said a deputy was injured trying to save them—I need his name."

"Why? Do you think it has something to do with the murder?"

My phone beeped while she was talking. I quickly glanced at the screen and saw that Melvin was trying to call in. I'd have to call him back. "I'm not sure. I just need his name."

"It was Justin, Justin Singleton. He works for..."

I nearly dropped my phone when Mallory said his name. I know she was still talking, but everything she said was a murmur. My mind raced and my mouth went dry. Why hadn't Justin mentioned knowing Lance? I'd seen the scar on his neck, but it wasn't my business. Should I have asked about it? He had handled most of the evidence in the case. Had he sabotaged it? I had so many questions and no answers. I needed to get my ass to Baton Rouge.

CHAPTER 39

Twenty minutes earlier…
Mechant Loup Fire Department

During the peer support group meeting, Melvin couldn't help but notice the sweat that had formed on Cole Peterson's forehead and the way he kept wringing his hands. The young fireman was clearly still troubled by the fire that took Lance Beaman's life. Melvin glanced at Stephanie. She had noticed, too, and was frowning as she studied Cole.

Not knowing what to say in support, Melvin had remained quiet throughout the meeting. Ox had done most of the talking and he had shared some personal experiences and self-help techniques that seemed to help Cole relax a little.

"Well," Ox finally said, "if there's nothing more, we can break for the evening. I've been trying to change a flat tire on Unit Four, so I didn't get to cook anything, but we have cookies in the kitchen."

"When's the next meeting?" Melvin asked, hoping it would be soon.

Ox pulled out his phone, checked his calendar. "We'll plan one for two Thursdays from now, if that's okay with everyone. We can meet sooner if necessary."

"That'll be good." Melvin glanced at Cole, who had walked toward the kitchen with the other six members who had shown up. Someone had made it to the cookie tray and was already eating one. As Ox headed to the garage, Melvin strode to the kitchen to say goodbye. "I've got to get to work," he said, shooting a thumb toward his uniform, "but I'll see y'all next time."

Stephanie smiled and waved after him as he headed for the door, then grabbed a chocolate chip cookie with each hand.

"Can I talk to you for a second?" Cole called out to him.

Melvin paused by the door and turned to see Cole heading toward him.

"In private," Cole said.

"Sure." Melvin led the way to the parking lot and walked to his loaner truck. He turned to face Cole, leaning his back against the driver door. "What is it?"

Cole shoved his hands in his pockets, shuffled his feet nervously. "I...I don't know if it means anything. I mean, it can't mean anything."

Melvin cocked his head to the side. "What are you talking about?"

"I overheard something and I didn't tell Detective Clint about it."

His curiosity thoroughly aroused, Melvin pushed off of the truck. "What is it, Cole? What did you overhear?"

Cole licked his lips. "I heard Jack Billiot tell his mom that Lance Beaman was driving a car that killed some young girls."

"Go on..."

"Well, that was the week before Beaman was killed. I...I thought it was a coincidence, but then I saw something today that scared the hell out of me." Cole jerked around and stared wildly about when the door to the fire department opened and the other members of the group exited, headed for their cars. He just stood there watching until they had all entered their vehicles and driven away. Once he was sure no one could hear him, he reached deep into his pocket and continued. "I saw this picture in the newspaper today"—he removed a rumpled paper and handed it to Melvin—"and I recognized that lighter."

Melvin sucked in his breath. Susan had told him about Clint sending the picture of the lighter to the *Mechant Voice*, but they'd both figured it wouldn't yield anything. "There are a thousand lighters like that, so I bet we'll get tons of false leads," Melvin had said. "But I sure hope it helps. I'm still pissed at the bastard who shot at me. I want a do-over."

"Are you sure you recognize it?" Melvin asked. "There're a million lighters like this."

"Not only do I know who it belongs to, but I know who killed Beaman."

"Who?" Melvin could feel his neck tighten. "Who is it, Cole?"

Cole licked his lips and glanced over his shoulder again. "My life could be in danger."

"Don't worry about that. I'll keep you safe."

"It's…um, it's Ox. Ox is the one who set fire to that man and he's the one who shot at you, because that's his lighter."

Melvin's knees grew weak, his hands started to sweat. He had not expected that answer. "Ox?" His voice was incredulous. "Are you sure?"

"He lied when Detective Clint asked us if Jack had said anything when we responded to his heart attack. Ox was standing right there next to me when Jack told his mom Beaman killed those girls, but he straight up lied. I started to tell the truth, but…" Cole let his voice trail off for a moment, then continued. "He gave me this look that scared the crap out of me, so I shut up. I know he'll kill me if he finds out I told on him."

The moment of shock passed quickly for Melvin. He felt his blood beginning to boil as he remembered how desperate he felt that night when the gunman—when Ox—was advancing on his position, slinging lead in his direction. "How sure are you that the lighter belongs to him?"

"I'm positive. Ox has said many times—" Cole abruptly spun around. "What was that noise?"

Melvin looked toward the building, shielded his eyes from the setting sun. He'd heard a noise, but had been blinded by the light and couldn't identify the source of the sound. All appeared secure at the moment. He shrugged. "It could be an alley cat or something. Go back to your story."

Cole hesitated, then sighed. "So, Ox said his dad gave him that lighter. It was his dad's lucky lighter. He said it kept his dad safe all through Vietnam, so his dad gave it to him when he got back from the war."

Cole shot a thumb over his shoulder. "I know it's his lighter because I've never seen him light a cigarette with anything else— until we responded to Beaman's fire. After we had put out the fire and were waiting for Detective Clint to get there, Ox went to light a cigarette and couldn't find his lighter. Someone else had to give him a light. Ever since then he's been using those cheap plastic jobs."

Cole was still talking, but Melvin was no longer listening. "I want you to get in your car and get out of here," Melvin said. "And don't come back."

Cole hesitated. "What're you going to do?"

"My job." After Cole got in his car and started it, Melvin walked to his truck and pulled his gun belt from the floorboard, where he'd left it with his ballistics vest. He slung the gun belt around his waist, then snatched his cell phone from his pocket and called Clint. It rang several times before going to voicemail. "Clint, this is Melvin. Ox is the one who killed Beaman. He's inside the fire department garage changing a flat tire. I'm going to keep him occupied, but I won't confront him unless it's absolutely necessary. Come as quick as you can."

CHAPTER 40

Melvin strode quickly across the meeting area of the fire department and paused by the rear entrance to the garage, hitched up his belt. After taking a deep breath, he stepped through the doorway and scanned the room. He saw Ox squatting over a tire.

"Hey, Ox, what's up?" He tried to sound as relaxed as possible. "Need a hand?"

"This tire's what's up." Ox glanced in Melvin's direction. "I thought you had to go to work."

"I do, but I saw everyone leave, so I wanted to lend a hand. I also wanted to thank you for putting these meetings together. They've really helped out a lot."

"That's why I'm here, Melvin...to help others." Ox fixed him with a steady gaze. "Everything I do is for the good of this community. I've spent my entire life giving to the people of Chateau and Mechant Loup." He pointed to the scars across his face. "I've given sweat, tears, blood, and flesh for these people."

Melvin nodded. "Yeah, you have. And we all appreciate it."

"I don't know, Melvin." Ox turned to study the flat tire in front of him. "It seems some people don't appreciate all I've given and sacrificed for this place. It seems some people just want to hurl out accusations and tarnish a good man's reputation."

Melvin inched a little closer, allowing his hand to dangle near his firearm. Ox froze in place, and Melvin knew the fireman sensed his movement.

"No one doubts your service to the community," Melvin said slowly, trying to keep the anger from his voice. "I, for one, really appreciate everything you do."

What I don't appreciate, Melvin thought, *is your cowardly ass trying to ambush me!*

Ox turned slowly on the stool atop which he sat and lifted his cold eyes in Melvin's direction. It was only then that Melvin noticed the gun that Ox was holding. It was a 9 mm semi-automatic pistol and it dangled loosely in Ox's right hand.

"I heard what Cole told you." Ox's voice was lethal. "You didn't come back here to thank me or to shoot the shit. You came here to arrest me, didn't you?"

Although Melvin's heart was racing, his demeanor exuded calmness and confidence. "Why would I arrest you, Ox?"

"Don't play games with me. I already told you—I heard what Cole said to you out front."

Melvin tilted his head slightly, listening—hoping—for the sound of sirens in the distance. There was nothing. "If you really heard what Cole said to me and you think I need to arrest you, then you must've murdered Lance Beaman."

"I didn't murder anybody." Ox spat a stream of saliva against the side of the fire truck. "Lance deserved what he got for killing those poor girls and for making everyone think Carl Wainwright did it."

"And what gave you the right to pass judgment on him?"

"I didn't say it was me who passed judgment on him."

"It was you who taught Stephanie to imagine that her victims committed some God-awful sin in their past lives to help her get over the hurt she felt for them, wasn't it?"

"It works every time."

"What sin do you suppose I committed?" Melvin asked pointedly.

"Excuse me?" Ox appeared genuinely confused.

"You ambushed me, tried to murder me, so I'm wondering how you settled that within yourself. What sin did you imagine I committed to help you get over trying to murder a cop?"

"I already told you—I didn't try to murder anyone."

Melvin smirked. "You're such a coward."

Ox's knuckles turned white as he gripped the pistol tighter. "What did you say?"

"A real man would own what he did, not lie like a little bitch."

Ox lunged forward, and Melvin was ready for him. Knowing he didn't have time to draw his pistol before Ox would pull the trigger, Melvin shot his right foot forward and delivered a front kick to Ox's left wrist. Ox's hand shot upward and the pistol flew from his grasp. Melvin caught sight of the pistol for a brief moment and saw it disappear over the truck overhead.

Moving with lightning speed, Melvin reached for his own pistol. It had almost cleared the holster when Ox came up with the tire iron and aimed it at the left side of Melvin's head. Throwing his left arm up to protect his head, Melvin took the full force of the blow on the outside of his left bicep. He felt a sharp pain. A shock reverberated up and down his arm. He knew immediately that it was broken.

Wincing, Melvin swung his right hand around, trying to bring his pistol to bear on Ox. Before he could level it on the firefighter, Ox dropped the tire iron and grabbed a hold of Melvin's right hand with both of his, fighting to wrench the pistol free. Melvin held on for dear life. He shoved his left shoulder into the larger man and tried to knock him off his feet, but the fire truck caught him.

Ox grunted and grabbed Melvin's right pinky, jerked it upward. Melvin groaned as he heard the bone snap and felt pain shoot through his hand. Although he was in extreme pain, he was cognizant that he was losing his grip on the gun, and he knew that was his greatest danger at the moment.

Melvin realized he had no choice but to try and empty the pistol. Struggling to shove Ox off-balance, he smashed the magazine release button with his right thumb and the loaded magazine fell to the ground. Through the whirl of pain from his injured arm and pinky, he was able to glance down and locate the magazine on the smooth concrete. Shifting his weight briefly, he kicked out with his right foot and sent the magazine sliding somewhere under the fire truck.

Ox let go of the pistol with one hand and shoved a thumb in Melvin's left eye. Melvin cried out in pain and anger. His left arm was numb and his hand tingled, and he was unable to bring it up to protect himself. Afraid that Ox would eventually wrestle the pistol away from him, Melvin strained with all his might to turn the muzzle toward Ox and pulled the trigger.

The gunshot was deafening inside the metal garage. Melvin's ears rang. The gunshot surprised Ox and caused him to loosen his grip on Melvin's eye. Seizing the opportunity, Melvin twisted his head around and bit a chunk out of Ox's forearm.

"You little bastard!" Ox jerked his arm out of Melvin's mouth and punched Melvin right in the throat. Melvin's knees buckled and he collapsed to his knees. Ox kicked Melvin in the gut and Melvin doubled over, then slumped to his side on the ground.

Straining to breathe, Melvin glanced up at Ox. His left eye was blurry, so he closed it. He gasped when he saw Ox through his right eye reaching down and pulling a large survival knife from his boot. It was at least ten inches long and light from the ceiling glinted on the silver blade.

Ox planted the heel of his boot against Melvin's left shoulder and shoved him flat on his back. Melvin tried to scoot away from Ox, but the firefighter stomped him in the groin. Melvin grunted, paralyzed from the pain.

"I'm not going to jail today or any day," Ox mumbled, dropping to his knees, straddling Melvin's chest. Lifting the knife high in the air, Ox took a deep breath and paused for a brief moment, staring straight into Melvin's eyes. Unable to speak, Melvin shook his head slowly, begging Ox to reconsider. As he waited for the man to make his decision, images of Claire and Delilah flashed through his mind. A wave of panic washed over him, and he wondered if he would ever see his wife and baby again.

"Please...don't," he managed to say, but it didn't sound like his voice. "I've got a wife and daughter. They...they need me."

"You should've thought about that before you walked into my building and tried to take me in." Ox gritted his teeth and, letting out a ferocious yell, brought the knife down on Melvin.

CHAPTER 41

East Main Street

"It's Ox!" I hollered to Susan, my phone pinned to my ear as I took the turn onto the bridge that connected the east side of Mechant Loup with the west side. "And Melvin's gone after him!"

"Damn it!" I could hear Susan's boots echoing loudly and I knew she was running down the hallway at the office. "Are they still at the fire department?"

"Yeah...Ox is in the garage changing a flat." I turned onto Washington Avenue and raced toward Main Street. "I received a voicemail from Melvin saying he was going to keep him occupied until we get there."

"What's that supposed to mean?"

As I shot past the police department, I saw Susan backing out from under the building. Neither of us had our sirens on, as we didn't want to alert Ox. I was about to respond to Susan when the radio scratched to life and Lindsey called out.

"Chief, we just received a frantic call saying someone heard a gunshot inside the fire department." Lindsey's voice sounded strained. "And...and they think Melvin's in trouble."

I punched the steering wheel, begged my Tahoe to go faster. I smashed the brakes and jerked the steering wheel when I reached Main Street, heading south. Susan was right on my bumper. Within seconds, we were screeching into the parking lot of the Mechant Loup Fire Department and I saw Cole Peterson sitting on the ground behind his car. His head was in his hands and it appeared he was crying. His cell phone was on the ground beside him.

"Where's Melvin?" I asked when my Tahoe lurched to a stop and I jumped out.

Cole lifted his tear-streaked face and pointed toward the large garage attached to the fire department building. "They're inside. I heard a...someone fired a shot. I think he got Melvin!"

Gun in hand, I sprinted as fast as I could toward the entrance to the fire department. Susan was two steps ahead of me but she slowed when she hit the door, and we squeezed through, shoulder-to-shoulder. A quick scan of the meeting area showed it was clear. Susan pointed toward the doorway that connected the meeting area with the garage, and we raced for it.

We were twenty feet away when we heard a ferocious yell and then an agonizing howl. My heart pounded in my chest. The lights in the building seemed much brighter than they really were. The doorway in front of me seemed to sway up and down as I approached it, running as fast as my legs could carry me. When I pushed through the doorway with Susan and my eyes took in the scene before me, I nearly vomited.

Ox was straddling Melvin and he was using all of his body weight to plunge a large knife into my friend. The blade of the knife had gone through Melvin's palm and was sticking out of the back side of his hand. The tip was buried in his chest and it was being pushed toward his back. Blood poured from the hole in Melvin's hand and covered his face. He was grunting and squirming as he struggled desperately to save his own life.

I immediately pushed my Beretta 9 mm pistol forward and snapped off three shots. The 124-grain bullets entered the top of Ox's head and destroyed everything they touched on the other side of his skull. Before his body could react to the shots, Susan dove into him and knocked him sprawling, relieving the pressure of the blade from Melvin's chest.

Melvin's right hand collapsed and he lay there gasping for air. His eyes stared unseeing at the ceiling. I dropped my pistol and fell to his side, screaming for someone to call an ambulance. Susan was on her radio immediately. As I pressed my hands to Melvin's chest in an attempt to stop the bleeding, I felt the presence of other people starting to gather around us. Hands clutched at my shoulders and dragged me away from him as those more capable of fixing the wounded stepped in to help. In the ensuing blur of activity, I caught sight of Cole Peterson. The young boy, who had been trembling and crying near his vehicle only moments earlier, was now all business as he worked feverishly to save a good man, a great cop, and an excellent father.

It seemed like hours, but it had to be minutes, until a team of ambulance personnel rushed in and took over. I could tell by their actions and the way they spoke that it didn't look good. When I caught sight of Melvin's face through the bustling bodies, my heart sank and I panicked. His eyes were closed and the muscles in his face were completely relaxed.

I scanned the crowd of first responders, trying to find Susan. When I did locate her, she was standing across from where I sat. She was with Amy Cooke and they were both fighting back tears, but they were both losing that fight.

Tears clouded my own eyes as I watched what was taking place. Melvin was as loyal as they came and we couldn't lose him. I didn't know what this town would do without him. I didn't know what *I* would do without him.

Through the agony and fear that strangled me, I heard a voice breaking through the cloud. It sounded muffled, but, in all of the confusion, the message somehow resonated; "Clear a landing zone! He needs to be air-medded out of here!"

I saw Susan spring into action and I followed suit, wiping the tears from my eyes as we rushed outside. The parking lot was huge and would be an adequate LZ for the medical helicopter, but we had to clear out some cars first. I drove my Tahoe across the lot and into the grass beside the building, and then set about gathering keys to the other vehicles. With Susan's help, we cleared out the parking lot just in time to hear the chopping sounds of the helicopter approaching.

It was just making its descent when the medics came rushing out of the fire department, pushing a gurney in front of them. I stopped what I was doing and stood at attention, watching Melvin's figure closely. He was wrapped in a white sheet and the only thing I could see was his face. His eyes were still closed, his body seemed limp—

I jerked in my skin when I heard a shrill scream from the other side of Main Street. I spun in that direction and saw Melvin's wife sprinting across the highway, her nightgown flowing behind her like a cape as she ran.

"Amy!" Susan hollered, waving her arms wildly. "Get her! Stop Claire!"

Amy was standing on the centerline blocking traffic. She sprung into action and intercepted Claire before she could reach the helicopter. Claire was screaming and flailing her arms, fighting hard to break free from Amy's clutches. I could hear Amy telling her it would be okay, but I could hear in her voice she wasn't sure. She promised to drive Claire to the hospital to be with Melvin, but it didn't help. Claire was still fighting when the helicopter lifted off and began fading into the evening sky.

I looked upward and watched the large metal bird as it disappeared to the north, heading for a trauma center in New Orleans. I was aware of a hand in mine and someone standing beside me. I knew without looking that it was Susan.

"God, I hope he survives." She indicated with her head toward Claire, who had finally collapsed in a heap at Amy's feet. "For her sake and ours."

CHAPTER 42

Four hours later…

The large waiting room at the trauma center in New Orleans was crowded. Every Mechant Loup officer—Amy Cooke, Takecia Gayle, Baylor Rice, Susan and me—were huddled together in a corner of the room, along with our dispatchers, Lindsey, Marsha, and Beth. A dozen Chateau Parish sheriff's deputies had driven into the city to show their support, and five or six New Orleans officers were standing by the entrance in case we needed anything.

Claire was in a private room with her mother and one of her friends from work. The last we had heard, Melvin was in emergency surgery. He was bleeding internally—as well as externally—and he'd lost a lot of blood. One of his lungs had collapsed and his blood pressure had crashed. Secondary to the life-threatening injuries, he had a broken arm, a dislocated pinky finger, and what his doctors described as "bilateral pubic rami fractures". It sounded painful and was apparently the result of Ox stomping him in the groin area, and it would require surgery to fix.

The door that led from the emergency room to the lobby swished open and I heard excited chatter. I turned to look over my shoulder and saw Mayor Pauline Cain heading toward us. Sheriff Buck Turner was with her, and they were followed shortly by Justin Singleton.

"How's Melvin?" Pauline asked once she'd reached our location and given each of us a hug. "Is he going to be okay?"

I glanced at Susan, who frowned. "We don't know anything more than what we knew when we walked in…and it's not good."

Sheriff Turner offered his condolences. "Take care of whatever y'all need to take care of here," he said. "I sent a pair of deputies and a dispatcher to cover the town. They can stay as long as you need them."

Susan thanked him.

"And Mallory's running lead on the investigation out at the fire station." Turner indicated with his head toward Justin, addressed him. "Didn't you stop by and meet with her before coming here?"

I studied Justin coldly.

"Yeah, I did. She said Ox was dead on arrival, but"—Justin nodded toward me—"I'm sure you already knew that."

"We need to talk," I said sternly, then turned on my heel and headed for the door. I looked back once to make sure Justin was following me. Once we were out in the parking lot, I demanded to know why he never told me his connection to Lance Beaman.

He sighed heavily. "I didn't realize the connection. I remembered the names of the twins and I remembered Carl Wainwright's name, but that was only because I received an award and their names were mentioned at the ceremony. I didn't remember the names of the other passengers in the car until tonight. In fact, I don't think I ever knew their names. I ended up spending a couple of weeks in a burn unit in Baton Rouge, and by the time I recovered and went back to work it was old news."

I pursed my lips, pointed to his neck. "So, that's where you got the scars?"

"Yeah." His eyes seemed sad. "It's where Ox got his scars, too. He was with me when the explosion happened. We tried so hard to get those girls out, but...but we were too late. We both got burned pretty good and it took us out of the fight." He paused and shook his head. "His injuries were worse than mine. Not only did he spend more time in the burn unit, but he could never cover up his scars." He shook his head. "I still can't believe he did all of this, but I certainly understand why. I hated Carl Wainwright ever since that night, and if I would've found out it was Lance Beaman—hell, I can't promise I wouldn't have gone after him myself."

A thought suddenly occurred to me, and it was probably why I'd never suspected a fireman. "I thought you said it was an amateur job?"

"It was." He grunted. "Just because Ox was a firefighter, it doesn't mean he would've made a good anarchist. Firefighters are not skilled in making Molotov cocktails and killing people—they're trained to *save* people."

I shrugged, realizing he had a point. "Did you learn anything else when you met with Mallory?"

"Yeah, we interviewed Ox's wife. She said he fell into a deep depression after the fire. He was suicidal. She said it took years for him to get over it, but he finally did. She said he went years without talking about it and then, a few days before Lance was murdered, he went on a rage. She was in the kitchen, but she could hear him tearing up the garage. He was cursing and saying something about the wrong man dying. She heard him curse Lance and it took her by surprise, because he didn't know Lance."

"What'd she do when word got out about Lance's murder?"

"She confronted him, but he denied it. She said she could always tell when he was lying, and she knew he killed Lance."

"Why didn't she come forward?"

"He burned a man alive, Clint—you don't piss off a fellow like that."

I couldn't argue that point. Fear was a powerful deterrent.

"When she confronted him," Justin said, "he exploded. He punched a hole in the laundry room cabinet, flipped their China cabinet over, and told her she'd better never utter those words again."

I went over the entire case in my mind, wondering if there was any way we could have identified him earlier. I shuddered when I realized that, had it not been for Delvin Miller spitting on Lance's coffin, we might never have solved this case.

Wanting to be close by in case we got word from Melvin's doctors, I returned inside. I caught Pauline staring at me from where she was leaning against a wall, all alone, so I walked over. "How are you, Mayor?"

Her eyes and face were red and puffy. "Scared."

"We all are...but he's a fighter. He'll pull through." I didn't know how confident I sounded, but I certainly didn't feel it. I was terrified for Melvin. I'd seen lots of dead and dying people in my time, and Melvin didn't look good when I saw him last. After a moment of awkward silence, I apologized for suspecting her of murder. "I should've known better than to think you'd be involved with something like that."

She stared down at her feet. "Given my lack of candor, I can understand why you would suspect me. My only hope is that Melvin makes a full recovery. I just want all of this to be over and I want things to go back to normal."

"Me, too." My phone buzzed in my pocket. It was Mallory. I stepped away from Pauline and found an unoccupied corner of the waiting room. "This is Clint..."

The first thing she did was ask about Melvin.

I glanced toward the door where we'd last seen his doctor. "We're still waiting and praying. What've you got?"

"I just wanted to let you know we woke up the state firearms examiner and she agreed to take a look at Ox's pistol. It matched the shell casings that were recovered from Melvin's shooting. We also rolled Ox's prints and one of my guys compared it to the print from the lighter—it was a match." She paused for a breath, then told me they'd searched Ox's house and property and located materials to make a ton of Molotov cocktails and literature detailing how to do it. "There were enough bottles and fuel to start a mini war. We've packaged them and will bring them to the lab in the morning. I'm sure they'll match the same types of bottles and fuel that were used in Lance's attack."

When she was done talking, I thanked her and sought out Susan. I was still looking when we heard a long wailing cry come from the private room where Claire was waiting. My heart sank to my boots and I almost collapsed. The room began spinning. I stumbled forward, reaching out for the door long before I got to it. Someone bumped into me and I turned to see Susan, Amy, Baylor, and Takecia rushing forward. We were halfway to the door when it burst open and we saw Melvin's doctor standing there, looking haggard.

Every person in the waiting room turned their attention toward the doctor, everyone frozen in place. My heart stopped in my chest as I waited with bated breath. I could feel Susan's nails digging into my forearm.

The doctor cleared his throat, and we all flinched.

"He's...um, he's going to pull through. He'll make a full recovery." He continued talking, but his voice was drowned out as the room erupted in wailing cries and guttural displays of relief.

Unable to contain my emotions, I sank to my knees and wept, thanking God for saving my friend. It was the first time I'd ever cried because I was happy.

I don't know how long I knelt there, but I finally looked up to see Susan tugging on my arm. I stood slowly to my feet and walked with her to the parking lot. She told me the doctor said we couldn't visit Melvin until much later, so we decided to walk down the block to get some food. When we were done eating—I didn't have much of an appetite—we returned to the hospital and watched as everyone rotated out to get some food.

It wasn't until noon on the next day that Claire was finally able to visit with Melvin. When she came out to the waiting room—where we were all waiting anxiously—she was beaming.

"He's looking hungry," she declared, "but he's cracking jokes."

"He's always hungry," I said, relief wrapping over me like a warm blanket. I wanted to ask her if he planned on going back to work after he recovered, but I knew it was too early and it would be a selfish question. I had left the department for a year, yet here I was hoping Melvin would return to work as soon as possible. If he didn't, I would miss the big brute.

When Claire rejoined her family in the private waiting room, I turned to Susan and asked her if she thought he'd come back to work.

"You saw his blood," Susan said simply. "It was blue."

BJ Bourg

BJ Bourg is an award-winning mystery writer and former professional boxer who hails from the swamps of Louisiana. Dubbed the "real deal" by other mystery writers, he has spent his entire adult life solving crimes as a patrol cop, detective sergeant, and chief investigator for a district attorney's office. Not only does he know his way around crime scenes, interrogations, and courtrooms, but he also served as a police sniper commander (earning the title of "Top Shooter" at an FBI sniper school) and a police academy instructor.

BJ is a four-time traditionally-published novelist (his debut novel, JAMES 516, won the 2016 EPIC eBook Award for Best Mystery) and dozens of his articles and stories have been published in national magazines such as Woman's World, Boys' Life, and Writer's Digest. He is a regular contributor to two of the nation's leading law enforcement magazines, Law and Order and Tactical Response, and he has taught at conferences for law enforcement officers, tactical police officers, and writers. Above all else, he is a father and husband, and the highlight of his life is spending time with his beautiful wife and wonderful children.

http://www.bjbourg.com

Made in United States
Troutdale, OR
07/24/2025

33159098R00116